The Everyman Wodehouse

P. G. WODEHOUSE

# The Luck Stone

EVERYMAN

Published by Everyman's Library
50 Albemarle Street
London W1S 4BD

First published in *Chums* magazine, September 1908–January 1909
(under the pseudonym Basil Windham)
Copyright by The Trustees of the Wodehouse Estate
All rights reserved

Published by Everyman's Library, 2014

Typography by Peter B. Willberg

ISBN 978-1-84159-195-7

A CIP catalogue record for this book is available from the British Library

Distributed by Penguin Random House UK,
20 Vauxhall Bridge Road, London SW1V 2SA

Typeset by AccComputing, Wincanton, Somerset
Printed and bound in Germany
by CPI books GmbH, Leck

# The Luck Stone

# CONTENTS

It is not always pleasant to have the mumps. There are several drawbacks to the malady.

It can be painful, and it does not tend to improve one's personal appearance. But it has this great advantage, that, if it attacks you towards the end of the holidays, you are pretty certain to be enjoying yourself at home when the rest of the world has gone back to school.

This was the case with Jimmy Stewart. After six weeks of the best time imaginable, he had been informed by the doctor, just when the prospect of school was beginning to lose the vagueness which had surrounded it during August and the early part of September, that he had got the mumps, and would be unable to return to Marleigh for another three weeks. Jimmy had danced a cake-walk as a feeble attempt to do justice to his feelings.

It was not that he disliked Marleigh. As a school he was very fond of it. Still, there was no getting out of the fact that it was a school; and, with the weather as glorious as it was, Jimmy did not want any school.

So he went into quarantine with a light heart. The chief drawback to mumps – the fact that one is cut off from the society of one's fellows – did not worry Jimmy. He was a sociable youth in term-time, and had as many friends as anybody else in the school; but in the holidays he found his own company good enough for him. He liked to loaf about by himself by the river, reading and ratting and fishing, and mumps made no difference to this programme. His father, Colonel Stewart, of the Indian Army, had been big-game shooting in Africa for the last nine months, and when his father was away he never saw anybody to speak of during the holidays, except the servants.

So Jimmy with the mumps carried on much as he had done before he got the mumps. The weather kept fine, and he spent most of his time down by the river. It was now the last evening of his extra holidays. The doctor, to his disgust, had been up that morning, and pronounced him free from infection.

'You can go back to your school tomorrow,' he said.

'Wouldn't it be better if I took another day or two?' suggested Jimmy. 'It would be rather sickening for the chaps at Marleigh if I spread mumps there.'

'You're too unselfish, my lad,' said Doctor Willis. 'We mustn't have you depriving yourself of school for their sake. Back you go tomorrow by the first train!'

'Oh, dash,' said Jimmy.

'Just so,' said Doctor Willis.

Jimmy had spent his last evening in one long, last bathe in the pool below the mill. It was getting on for October, but the water was still warm; and Jimmy had splashed about for an hour. He was now lying on the bank, reading.

A shadow fell across his book. He looked up. A sturdy, brown-faced man was standing beside him. It was his brownness which struck Jimmy most in his appearance. He was more sunburnt than anyone he had seen, with the exception of his father. The Indian sun had tanned Colonel Stewart to the colour of walnut, and this man had the same dried-up look.

'Well, matey,' said the man.

'Hullo,' said Jimmy.

'Taking a spell off?'

'Yes.'

'Love us, it does a man good to see all this green. There's nothing to beat the good old English country. When you've been in India for half a dozen years—'

'I thought you came from India,' said Jimmy.

'The sun there ain't what you'd call a patent complexion cream, love us if it is. Do you live in these parts?'

'In the holidays I do.'

'Then perhaps you could tell me where a house by the name of Gorton Hall is. G-o-r-t-o-n. That's the place.'

Gorton Hall was Colonel Stewart's house. Jimmy wondered for a moment what the man might want there, but he supposed he must be a friend of one of the servants. In Colonel Stewart's absence the servants had developed a habit of entertaining to a certain extent. Friends from the village were always dropping in.

'It's straight on down the road at the end of this field. You could get to it by a short cut, but you'd probably miss your way. Better stick to the road. You go by the church, pass a public-house—'

'Do I!' said the other. 'Not if I know it. Not with a thirst like what I've got. Five minutes one way or the other won't make much difference to me now. So long, matey. Be good.'

'So long,' said Jimmy, returning to his book.

He read on for another hour and more, till the sun disappeared behind the mill, and a chilly mist from the river reminded him that it was not midsummer, when you could sit out of doors half the night. There was very little fun in sitting there, shivering;

so Jimmy got up, and began to walk back to the house across the fields.

It was dusk by the time he got into the drive. Everything looked dim and mysterious. The book Jimmy had been reading had been of a sensational type, and he could not keep down that vague feeling that someone was looking at him from behind his back, and following him, which most people have experienced at one time or another. He stopped now and then to listen, but he could hear nothing. He walked on quickly up the drive towards the house, where the lighted windows gleamed cheerfully.

Suddenly his heart leaped. A few feet in front of him a man's figure seemed to have appeared from nowhere. Jimmy stood still. Then he saw that the man was walking away from him, and a moment later he had recognised his friend of the riverside, the man from India.

'Rummy I didn't see him before,' thought Jimmy. 'I suppose the mist must have thinned.'

He hurried on to overtake the man. He was feeling that it would not be unpleasant to have company for what remained of the walk to the house. He broke into a trot.

The behaviour of the man in front was singular. He whipped round at the sound of footsteps, and when Jimmy arrived he found himself looking into the muzzle of a small black revolver.

The next moment the man had recognised him.

'Hullo, matey,' he said. 'It's you, is it? Thought it might be someone else. Excuse the gun, sonny. You get jumpy out where I've been, and you find it's best to get into the habit of being ready to shoot first, and challenge afterwards. But we're chums, we are. And what might you be after? What do you want at Colonel Stewart's house?'

'I live there,' said Jimmy, with a laugh. 'I'm his son, you know.'

The man looked at him with interest.

'His nipper, are you?' he said. 'Well, I expect you'll do him credit. He's a fine officer, the Colonel. Served under him in the North Surreys up on the frontier before I exchanged. He'll be in one of those rooms, I reckon,' he added, pointing to the lighted windows, 'dressing for mess.'

'Oh, no,' said Jimmy. 'Didn't you know? Father's not in England.'

'Not in England!'

The man looked dazed, almost as if he had received a blow.

'No. He's been out in Africa, shooting big game, for months. No one knows when he'll be back. I haven't had a letter from him for ages. He's not very good at writing. For all I know, he may be on his way back now.'

The man continued to stand staring blankly at him. It began to dawn on Jimmy at last that Colonel Stewart's absence was something that mattered more than a little.

'I'm awfully sorry,' he said. 'Had you to see him about something important?'

The man had opened his mouth to reply, when suddenly something hummed past Jimmy's ear like an angry wasp. The man from India reeled, staggered back, groping blindly with his hands, and fell in a heap.

## 2 THE MAN FROM INDIA — A FACE IN THE NIGHT

The suddenness of the thing paralysed Jimmy for the moment. It was all like a nightmare. He could not realise it. He had heard no report; he had seen no one. Yet there was the man on the ground, while a thin, dark stream trickled slowly over the gravel of the drive.

Then he found his voice and regained the use of his limbs simultaneously. He ran, shouting, towards the house.

As he reached it, the front door opened, throwing a flood of light out into the mist.

'Who's that? What's the matter? Lord, Master Jimmy, is that you?'

It was Perks, the Colonel's butler.

'Perks, there's a man been shot in the drive.'

Perks' was one of those minds which work slowly.

'Who shot him?' he inquired.

'I don't know. It all happened in a second. I was standing talking to him, when he went down in a heap. I heard the bullet. It whizzed close to my ear. But I didn't hear any shot. Come and help carry him in.'

'Is he dead, Master Jimmy?'

'I don't know. He looks jolly beastly.'

'I'll fetch George to help.'

Perks was beginning to feel uneasy about the affair. His had been a placid life up till now, and, if he had to roam about while assassins were in the offing, he felt that it would be just as well to have George, the groom, a man of muscle, by his side.

'Someone ought to fetch the doctor, Master Jimmy.'

Jimmy had a struggle with himself. He would have liked, above all things, to have stayed in the house, where everything was bright and lit-up and safe, instead of venturing out again into the darkness; but he told himself that it must be done, and he was the one who could do it quickest.

'I'll go,' he said. 'You bring the man in.'

He found his bicycle, and lifted it down the steps on to the drive. As he did so, George the groom appeared with Perks, carrying the board which was to act as a stretcher. They proceeded down the drive to where the man was lying, a vague shape in the darkness. Jimmy lit his lamp, and mounted. He slowed down as he reached the wounded man.

'How is he?' he asked.

George the groom touched his forelock.

'He ain't dead, Master Jimmy, but he's next door to it. If I was you I'd fetch the doctor quick.'

Jimmy rode on, looking neither to right nor left. He was conscious of a feeling as if a cold hand had been laid on the pit of his stomach, and his scalp was tingling. He had felt the same sensations before, in a slighter degree, on going in to bat for the school in an important match. If he had had to describe his feelings, he would have said that he was in a blue funk.

Once out of the drive and in the road, he felt better. It was not a long ride to the doctor's house. He propped his bicycle against the wall, and rang the bell. The doctor was in. Jimmy was shown into the consulting-room, and presently Doctor Willis entered, in cricket flannels, a Norfolk jacket, and carpet slippers, smoking a pipe.

'Well, young man,' he said, 'what do you mean by coming breaking in on an overworked medical man's hard-earned leisure? Have you come to tell me you've developed some other fatal malady which will keep you away from school?'

'I say, can you come up to the house at once? A man's been shot.'

'Been shot!'

'Yes. In our drive.'

'How did it happen?'

'I don't know. I was standing, talking to him, when the bullet came from nowhere, and hit him.'

'How do you mean – from nowhere? Didn't you hear a report?'

'No. That's the rummy part of it.'

'Where is he shot?'

'I don't know. I didn't stop to look. I rushed to the house to get help, and then came straight to you. Can you see him now?'

'I'll get my bicycle. Wait a moment.'

The moment seemed hours, but he reappeared at last, wheeling a bicycle and carrying a small bag.

'Now then,' he said.

They rode off together.

Perks was waiting at the door with the information that the wounded man had been placed on the sofa in the Colonel's sitting-room.

'You wait here, young man,' said Doctor Willis.

Jimmy sat down, and tried to interest himself in a book, but his brain was in a whirl, and he could not fix his attention on the print.

Presently he heard the sound of returning footsteps. Dr Willis came in, looking grave.

'It's been a nasty job,' he said. 'I've got it out, though.'

He held up a small piece of lead.

'Where was he hit?'

'In the left shoulder. An inch or two lower, and it would have been through his heart. Your friend has had a narrow escape. Who is he?'

'I don't know.'

'Don't know? He seems to know you. He's asking to see you.'

'I told him who I was. He'd come to see father. He'd served under him in India. I believe it was something important he wanted to see him about. At any rate, he looked jolly sick when I said father was away, and nobody knew when he'd be back.'

'Well, he wants to see you about something, and pretty badly, too. He wouldn't tell me what it was. Said he must see you. "Send the Colonel's nipper here," he kept saying.'

'I'd better go at once, hadn't I?'

Doctor Willis looked thoughtful.

'Strictly speaking,' he said, 'he isn't in a condition to see anyone. But he seems set on it, and it'll be worse for him if he worries. I've told him you'll be with him in a few minutes. This is a confoundedly mysterious affair, young man. I can't make it out. He seems to take it quite as a matter of course that he should have been shot through the shoulder with an air-gun in the drive of an English house. Yes, an air-gun. Not the sort you use. Something a great deal bigger and more dangerous. I should like to find the owner of that gun, and ask him one or two questions. There's too much mystery about this business to please me. Well, you'd better go and see him. You must not let him keep you long. He's very weak indeed. I shall give you a quarter of an hour; then out you'll have to come, whether he's told you what he wants to or not. Run along.'

Jimmy made his way to the sitting-room. The man was lying on the sofa, with his coat off and half his shirt cut away. His left shoulder was a mass of bandages. A shaded lamp burned on the table.

'Hullo,' said Jimmy awkwardly. The atmosphere of a sickroom always made him feel awkward.

'Well, sonny,' whispered the man. His voice was painfully weak, and the brown of his face had changed to a light yellow. 'Here! Pull that blind down.'

Jimmy looked at the window.

'There isn't one,' he said. A dislike of blinds was one of Colonel Stewart's fads. He detested anything that gave him a shut-in feeling.

'Never mind. I expect they'd be afraid to risk it.'

'Was there anything you wanted to tell me?' said Jimmy. 'The doctor says he'll only give us a quarter of an hour.'

'I won't waste time. I tell you, it gave me a bad shock when you told me the Colonel wasn't at home. Worse shock than that bloomin' bullet did, 'cos I was expecting that, and I wasn't expecting the other.'

'You were expecting it!'

'Yes, or something of the same sort. Do you know how many miles I've come to see the Colonel, sonny?'

'No.'

'No more do I. Thousands. And to find he wasn't on the spot when I got here. I tell you, it didn't want a bullet to knock me over then. A feather would have done it easy.'

'But how do you mean you were expecting it?'

'Because it's happened before. I've heard the whistle of those bullets half a dozen times, I have, since I left the Dâk Bungalow. Heard 'em zipping past my ears for all the world like blanked mosquitos in the 'ot weather. The day I left India one of 'em lifted the 'at off my head as if it was a breath of wind. It's like my luck that they should get me when I was thinking I was safe home. Pipped on the post, I call it.'

'Who are they?' whispered Jimmy.

'Never you mind, sonny. No one you'd know. I'm not sure I know myself, though I can make a pretty fair guess. They're modest, retiring coves, they are. Don't shove themselves forward. Would rather you didn't make a fuss over them, if it's all the same to you. Oh, they're beauties. I wish I could get within arm's reach of them. They'd get one of those unsolicited testimonials the papers are always writing about.'

His voice died away.

'Got a sip of water about, sonny?' he whispered.

There was a jug and a glass on the table. Jimmy poured out a glassful. He drank it greedily.

'Ah!' he grinned; 'there's a deal to be said for water, after all, though I was never one to take it at the canteen. Now, sonny, time's getting on. The doctor'll be coming in presently. I'll tell you what it is I wanted to say to you. Just fetch that coat there, will you? Got it? That's right. Now feel along the right sleeve. Inside. Ah! Feel anything?'

'There's a sort of hard lump.'

'Right you are, matey. There is a sort of hard lump. Now just you turn that sleeve inside out. Got a knife? Right. Cut the lining, and let's see what we've got.'

Jimmy did as he was directed. Something small and round dropped out into his hand. He looked at it curiously in the lamp-light. It was a dull, dirty blue stone. One side of it was half covered with a piece of brown paper, the other with some curious scratches, arranged with a certain order that suggested that they might be letters of some alphabet which was unknown to him. The stone was about the size of a shilling, perhaps a little larger; and it looked like nothing more than a piece of blue sealing-wax which had half melted, and, while in that condition, had got things stuck on to it.

Jimmy dropped the coat, and looked up. As he did so, something in the window caught the corner of his eye. He wheeled round.

A man's face was looking through into the room.

For a second Jimmy met his eyes. Then the face disappeared. He rushed to the window. There was nothing to be seen. The whole thing

might have been a trick of the imagination, so suddenly had it vanished. But Jimmy knew that his imagination had played him no trick. He had seen a man's face, a striking face, with piercing, cruel eyes. The lower half had been covered by a beard. He paused irresolutely.

'What's the matter, sonny?' asked the man on the sofa.

Jimmy pulled himself together. He remembered what Dr Willis had said about his patient's weak state. It was no good exciting him by telling him what he had seen. In his present state it might be dangerous.

'It's nothing,' he said; 'I only thought I heard something.'

The man sank back again on the sofa.

'They wouldn't risk coming so close to the house, not after what's happened,' he said. 'I expect it was nothing. Got the stone, matey?'

'Here you are,' said Jimmy, dropping it into his hand. The man looked at it in silence.

'Well,' he said at last, 'it ain't much of a thing, not to look at, is it? But it's a deal more important than it looks, that dirty little bit of blue glass is. It's cost a good few poor chaps their lives in its time, not forgetting a few narrow squeaks to Corporal Sam Burrows, which is me, matey. And too bloomin' nearly the late Corporal Sam Burrows for my taste. It's cruel hard luck, strike me if it ain't, not finding the Colonel here to take this bit of blue misery off my hands. See here, sonny. Listen to me. You're a good plucked one. I can see that. You're the Colonel's nipper, and you do him credit. Are you game to tackle what may turn out a nasty job?'

'What is it?'

'It's like this. There's certain parties what is most uncommonly anxious, as you see, to lay their hands on this stone. And there's certain other parties, what may be the Government of India or may not – I'm not telling you anything, mind – what's equally bloomin' anxious to keep it out of their hands till they can slip it over to the Colonel, who'll know what to do with it. See? Well, it's like this. It's no good me keeping the thing. They know where I am, and they'd have it in a couple o' days. But if you was to take it off to school with you, 'ow are they to know? They sees you going back to school, same as any other young gentleman. 'Ow are they to know you've got the blue ruin in your trousers' pocket? Though, mind you, there's always the risk. You've got to think of that. If these parties I'm talking about once got to know as how you'd got it, they'd be down on you like a swarm of bees. And bees with bloomin' A1 stings, too.'

Jimmy was silent. Things seemed to be happening to him so rapidly that everything had become unreal. Nothing sensational had ever occurred to him before in his whole life. His mind could only grasp one thing clearly, and that was that it was of the utmost importance that this small blue stone should be kept hidden till the return of Colonel Stewart. As for the risk – he could not forget the face that had looked into the room. Whoever had been at the window had seen him with the stone in his hands.

'Well, sonny?' said Sam Burrows.

The Stewarts, father and son, did not belong to the type which weighs every risk and chance of an adventure before embarking on it. They were accustomed to act first, and reckon up the danger afterwards. Colonel Stewart had won the D.S.O. for capturing a position which, according to all the rules of warfare, could not have been captured with the force at his disposal; and Jimmy took after his father.

'All right,' he said. 'Give us it.'

'You are the Colonel's nipper,' said Sam, with conviction. 'Here's the stone, sonny. Don't let it out of your hands for a minute. And keep your eyes skinned. Maybe there won't be any trouble at all, but if they do find out as you've got it – I wish I could tell you who to watch out for, but I bloomin' well don't know myself. I only 'eard their blanked bullets. I can tell you one thing, though. If you should see a brown man with a twisted leg hanging about, keep your eyes open, and don't go for walks without 'avin' a chum or two with you. He's the only one of the lot as I could swear to, and I don't know if he's in England. I 'ad dealings with him in India frequent, but whether he stopped there or not I couldn't tell you. I know I haven't set eyes on him this side. Hullo, here's the doctor come to tell you it's time for us to part.'

'You're perfectly right,' said Doctor Willis, taking Jimmy by the shoulder, and pushing him towards the door. 'There are your marching orders, young man; and if I catch you in here again, I'll give you the stiffest black draught you ever had.'

Jimmy did not sleep much that night. The excitement by itself
would have kept him awake. Added to the responsibility of
having the blue stone in his possession, it effectually put an end
to any hopes he might have had of dropping off. After lying
in the dark for an hour or so, he lit the gas, and began to read.
It was a slow business, and after a while he found it a hungry
one. At about three o'clock he was feeling that, if he did not get
something to eat at once, exhausted Nature would be able to
hold out no longer. He slipped on a coat and a pair of shoes, and
stole out.

He had been on these nocturnal expeditions before, both at
home and at school, where he and his friend, Tommy Armstrong,
made rather a habit of wandering by night. He knew that the
silence was the chief thing that made for success, even at home,
for Perks had a rooted objection to having his stores raided,
and Perks, when offended, could make himself thoroughly
objectionable.

So Jimmy crept quietly along till he reached the larder door.
It was only secured by a bolt outside. He went in, and was
rummaging about with the aid of a match when he heard a sound.

He blew out the match and listened intently. He had not
been mistaken. Somebody was trying to force open the pantry

window. He could hear the soft grating of a file against the catch. Whoever it was must have been busy for some time; for, as Jimmy waited, listening, the file completed its work, and the window was raised noiselessly inch by inch. Jimmy could see nothing distinctly, till a gleam of light cut through the darkness, as the unseen visitor opened his lantern.

The sight of the light brought Jimmy to himself.

What followed seemed funny to him when he recalled it later; but at the moment the humorous side of the thing did not appeal to him. His heart was beating wildly, as he groped out for something to throw. His fingers closed on a loaf of bread. He could just see the dim outline of a man's figure against the open window; and, aiming at a venture, he flung his loaf of bread with all the force at his disposal. There was a dull bump, followed by a yell and a clatter, as the lantern fell to the ground. He had evidently made a good shot.

The burglar, on receipt of the bread, had not waited for more. It was plain that he looked on houses where quartern loaves flew at him from nowhere as unsuitable for his purposes. Jimmy heard his footsteps retreating across the lawn. He went to the pantry window, and looked out. There was too much mist for him to see anything distinctly. But he was certain the man was gone.

He wondered what he had better do. If he gave the alarm, it would only lead to a great deal of confusion, and spoil the rest of a number of people who disliked having their sleep disturbed. It would do no good. The man was not likely to return, knowing that he had once been seen. So Jimmy, having closed the shutters – which should have been done before by Perks – lit another match, collected a plateful of biscuits and some apples, and went back to bed, where, at about half-past four, he managed to get to sleep.

\* \* \*

The train which was to take him back to Marleigh started at eleven o'clock. George the groom took him down in the dogcart, and Perks gave him a farewell benediction and a lunch-basket on the front steps.

Jimmy always rather liked the journey back to school. Perks seldom failed to come out strong with the food; and on the present occasion everything was in the best taste, notably a couple of bottles of home-brewed ginger beer, of a strength which beat anything he had come across previously.

Whether it was the lack of rest he had had during the night or the potency of the ginger beer, he did not know; but after half an hour an overwhelming feeling of drowsiness came over Jimmy. He could not keep his eyes open.

The next thing he was aware of was a dream-like sensation of seeing the well-known face of Tommy Armstrong at the open window.

It was so absolutely impossible that Tommy should be there that Jimmy could not realise that he was awake. To start with, Tommy was at Marleigh. And, even if he had not been, how could he possibly be outside the carriage?

At this moment the dream-figure spoke.

'Hullo, Jimmy,' it said. 'Lend a hand, will you, and lug me in.'

Jimmy shook off the last remnants of sleep and jumped up. Seizing Tommy by the hand, he hauled him into the carriage. As he did so, he was aware that the train was slowing down. It stopped just as Tommy, having rolled off the seat on to the floor, sat up and began to dust himself.

Tommy Armstrong was a freckled, red-haired youth with one of the widest grins ever seen on human face. He was about the same age as Jimmy. They shared a room at Marleigh. Tommy had the reputation of being the most reckless boy who had ever been to Marleigh School. He had absolutely no respect of persons, and why it was that the authorities had not dropped

heavily on him before now nobody could understand. Probably it was because, in addition to his recklessness, he possessed also, and could, when he pleased, exhibit a wonderful charm of manner. The German master, Herr Steingruber, whose life must have been a burden to him through Tommy, was never proof against it. He would set him colossal impositions during school hours, but, as often as he did so, he would cancel them as the result of a few minutes' conversation with the erring one after school was over. Tommy had a way of asking Herr Steingruber to play the 'cello, to which instrument the German master was devotedly attached, which was always good for a reprieve, whatever the offence may have been.

'What on earth's up?' asked Jimmy, as the train, with a jarring of brakes, came to a standstill. 'What the dickens were you doing outside there?'

'I wasn't outside there,' replied Tommy calmly. 'Get that idea right out of your head. Whatever else you may forget, remember that I have been in here with you the whole time. See? Don't forget, a financial ruin stares me in the eyeball. I shall have to sell my yacht and aeroplane.'

'What are we stopping for, I wonder!'

'Me. Don't give it away. They'll probably be round here in a jiffy.'

'Who?'

'The guard and his crew.'

'But why? What's happened?'

'I pulled the communication-cord.'

'What! What on earth for?'

Tommy sighed.

'I'm blowed,' he said, 'if I can tell you. It was like this. I was alone in the carriage, and that rotten advertisement of theirs about pulling the communication-cord kept catching my eye. I have always wondered what would happen if you did pull it, and after a bit I simply couldn't stand it any longer, so I just got up and gave the thing a tug. Well, then it struck me that I hadn't got five pounds to pass over to them when they came round, so I just nipped out of the window and shuffled along, trying to find an empty carriage. Hullo, here they are! I say, guard, what on earth are we stopping for?'

'Someone's bin and pulled the communication-cord.'

'What's up? A murder?'

'Someone's bin 'avin' a lark with the company, that's what's happened. It's a lark wot'll cost them five pounds, if I found 'oo it was did it.'

'Well, what's the matter with asking the people in the carriage where the cord is?'

'There ain't nobody there.'

'Are we going to stop here all night while you're hunting for the ghost?'

'I don't want none of your lip. I shouldn't be 'arf surprised if it wasn't you wot did it.'

'Don't be silly, my good man. Pull yourself together. How could I do it from here? Do you think I've got an india-rubber arm?'

'I don't know about that. You've got cheek enough for 'arf a dozen.'

'Go away,' said Tommy coldly. 'I don't like your face. I never did.'

By this time passengers' heads, protruding from windows, were demanding angrily the cause of the delay. The guard, grumbling, returned to his carriage, and soon afterwards the train started again.

'What on earth are you doing here?' asked Jimmy. 'Why aren't you at school?'

'Got a day off to go and see an uncle of mine, who lives down the line. Good old sort. Gave me a quid. It'll come in useful this term for paying off tick, and other things. Well, what's been the matter with you? What have you been slacking at home for all this while?'

'Mumps.'

'You look all right now.'

'I am. What's been happening at Marleigh?'

'Nothing much. Old Steingruber's been in pretty good form. He's taken up golf. He's a bit rottener at it than he is at anything else, which is saying a good deal. You remember him at cricket last term. Well, his golf's worse than that. He plays with Spinder. Oh, you don't know Spinder. He's a new master, and the most awful blighter you ever struck. Specs, hooked nose, getting bald on the top. Frightfully strict. Gives you beans if you do a thing. My life's been a perfect curse since he arrived. I'm dashed if I know what to do about it. I've only just worked off five hundred lines he gave me simply for letting a rabbit loose in form. It was one of Simpson's rabbits. He's got a couple. We take 'em up to the dormitory at night, and race them in the corridor. Awful sport. They're called Blib and Blob. Blib was the one I let loose in the form-room. Spinder collared it, only he gave it to the boot-boy, and I got it back for one-and-six. What have you got in that basket? Great Scott! Cake! Why didn't you tell me?'

Tommy suspended conversation for the moment, while he finished Jimmy's lunch.

Jimmy was thinking. Sam Burrows had told him not to let anyone know about the blue stone; but surely, he thought, he need not include Tommy. He was beginning to find the possession of the secret something of a strain. It would be a relief to confide in Tommy.

'I say,' he said.

'Hullo!' said Tommy, his mouth full of cake. 'I say, where do you get this cake? It's the best I ever bit. Keep me well supplied with it. You ought to study my tastes more. If only I had plenty of this sort of stuff I should be happy and contented all the time, instead of gloomy and a nuisance to everyone.'

'I say, Tommy, look at this.'

He fished the stone up from his pocket. Tommy examined it without much enthusiasm.

'I don't think much of it. What is it?'

'A precious stone of some sort, I think.'

'Let's have it for a second.' Tommy took possession of the stone, and tried to write his initials on the carriage window.

'It's a fraud,' he said, with conviction. 'If it was a precious stone, it would scratch glass. You've been had, my lad. Where did you get the rotten thing? How much did you give for it? It looks like a bit of sealing-wax.'

'I didn't give anything for it. It was given me to keep by a chap. He had come all the way from India to hand it over to my father, who's away. So he gave it to me instead, and I'm to let father have it directly he comes back. And, I say, Tommy, swear you won't say anything about it to a soul.'

'Why should I? And why not, if it comes to that?'

'Because it'll be frightfully dangerous for me if anybody gets to know I've got it. There's a gang of chaps after it, and they'll stick at nothing.'

'Pile it on.'

'I'm not rotting. It's a fact. I'm blowed if I know what there is about the stone that should make it so valuable – as you say, it looks pretty rotten, but I know it is valuable. The chap who gave it me was shot by the other chaps I was telling you about.'

'Shot! What, killed?'

'No. Shot through the shoulder. We were talking in our drive at the time. He told me that he'd been shot at heaps of times since he first got the stone. He's a chap called Burrows, a soldier. He'd served under my pater in India.'

Tommy looked searchingly at him.

'Look here, Jimmy, are you trying to pull my leg? Because

if you are, I'll roll you under the seat and chuck you out of the window.'

'I swear I'm not. It's all absolutely true.'

'Well, it's jolly rum. I don't see anything in the stone which would make anybody want it. Unless he was a lunatic. Perhaps that's it. Perhaps a lot of loonies from an asylum are after it. Anyhow, you can have it back. I've no use for it.'

Jimmy replaced the stone in his pocket. He had hardly done so when the train slowed down and halted at a small station. The door of the carriage opened, and a man in a brown suit got in, and settled himself in the corner opposite to Jimmy.

But for the fact that the man had a black eye, or rather a bruised eye, Jimmy might not have given him a second look. But a black eye is always picturesque, and demands a closer inspection. So Jimmy looked at him again, and a curious feeling of having seen him before somewhere came upon him.

Their eyes met, and then Jimmy's heart gave a leap. He had remembered. The face was the same face which had gazed at him through the window when he had seen the blue stone for the first time.

What did it mean? Could the man know? If not, why should he be shadowing him? Perhaps it was all a mistake. This might not be the same man. And yet Jimmy was convinced that it was. He had worn a beard then, and now he was clean-shaven. But the eyes were the same.

As these thoughts raced through Jimmy's mind, Tommy Armstrong broke the silence.

'I say, Jimmy,' he said, 'let's have another look at that stone.'

Jimmy saw the man in the corner give a slight start, and for a moment he felt physically sick.

'What are you talking about?' he faltered.

But Tommy, all unconscious, went on.

'Don't be an ass,' he said. 'You know what I mean. That rummy blue stone, that what's-his-name – Burrows gave you. I want to have another look at it.'

There was nothing to be done. If he refused to produce the stone, it would do no good. Tommy's remark had shown the man opposite the one thing which he had wanted to know, namely, that what he was seeking had left Sam Burrows' possession, and was now with Jimmy. He was not likely to risk an actual attempt to take it by force in a carriage of a train which was due to stop at another station in a few minutes. He would be content to have got on the trail of the thing, and to wait for a favourable opportunity before attempting to recover it.

Jimmy saw him flash a covert glance at the stone, as he passed it to Tommy; but, after that one glance had satisfied him that what Jimmy had got was what he was seeking, he closed his eyes and apparently went to sleep.

Tommy turned the stone over in his hand for a few minutes, then gave it back with a repetition of his former verdict.

'I call it pretty rotten,' he said. 'I'm blowed if I see what all the fuss is about. I wouldn't give twopence for the thing. Hullo, here we are.'

Not many people, as a rule, got out at Marleigh Station. It was a small station, used mostly by the boys of the school.

Jimmy more than half expected to see the man in the corner get out, but to his surprise he did not. The train rolled on, with him inside it, to all appearances still wrapped in sleep. Jimmy heaved a sigh of relief, then turned on Tommy.

'You are an idiot, you know,' he said. 'I particularly told you not to say a word about that stone to anybody.'

'Well, I didn't.'

'You made me bring it out in front of that man.'

'Oh, he didn't notice. He was asleep.'

'He pretended to be afterwards, but he was jolly wide awake when I was showing the stone. And I believe it was the man himself.'

'What man?'

'The man whose face I saw at the window, and who tried to break into the house.'

'What on earth are you talking about?'

'Why, didn't I tell you? When I was looking at the stone for the first time – it was in my pater's den, where Sam Burrows had been put on a sofa – I happened to glance up, and saw a man's face glaring at me through the window. And I could almost swear it was this chap.'

'What happened?'

'He dashed away. When I got to the window there was no one there.'

'You probably imagined the whole thing.'

'Did I? Well, I'll tell you a thing I didn't imagine, and that was going down to the larder in the middle of the night to get something to eat, and finding someone breaking into the house.'

'Great Scott, what did you do?'

'I picked up a loaf of bread, and shied it at him. It was pitch dark, but it got him all right. He dropped his lantern, and legged it. Did you notice that that man in the carriage had a black eye?'

'Yes. But he might have got that in a dozen different ways. It doesn't prove anything.'

'No. But it makes it beastly suspicious.'

'Oh, rot. And I'll tell you a thing which absolutely dishes your theory. If that man was your man, and he wanted to get the stone, and knew that you'd got it, why didn't he get out at Marleigh instead of going on?'

'Yes, there's something in that,' said Jimmy.

'Something in it? Of course, there is. It absolutely knocks the bottom out of your idea. If he'd really been after that stone, do you think he wouldn't have stuck to you like glue, and never let you out of his sight? You're all right. All you've got to do is to sit tight and not worry, until your pater comes back again.'

Jimmy agreed, feeling easy in his mind for the first time since he had set eyes on the man in the corner.

'I'll tell you what you can do, if you like,' Tommy went on. 'If you think there's any danger of your being suspected of having the stone, let me freeze on to it. They can't possibly think that I've got it, so that if you get waylaid and sandbagged by assassins, and all that sort of rot, they'll get jolly well left, because they won't be able to find the stone. They'll probably give it you jolly hot by way of getting a bit of their own back, but you'll have to lump that. You'll have the consolation of knowing your precious bit of blue sealing-wax is all right; and what's a whack over the head with a bludgeon if your mind's at rest? Sling the thing across.'

Tommy was looking on the whole business as an elaborate attempt on Jimmy's part to enliven the monotony of school life with a little added excitement and romance. He treated the matter as an amusing game. He had a matter-of-fact mind, and he did not believe in the existence of mysterious assassins outside the pages of sensational fiction. Whether Jimmy himself believed all he said, he did not know. To him it seemed that everything that had happened could be explained away simply and easily on common-sense lines. The shot that had struck down Sam Burrows – an accident. A spent bullet, perhaps, from some gun fired at a great distance. That would account for the absence of a report. The face at the window – imagination. The nocturnal visitor – simply an ordinary, conventional burglar, on the hunt for silver spoons like any other member of his profession.

The game, however, was very exciting, and he was prepared to do anything that lay in his power to help it on. It would be something to think about in school, when lessons became a bore.

His offer startled Jimmy. It offered an ingenious escape from the difficulties of the position. Jimmy had all his father's contempt for actual physical danger. All he desired was to fulfil the trust which had been placed in him by Sam Burrows, and keep the stone safe until his father's return to England. It seemed to him that for Tommy to become temporary guardian of the stone was to ensure its safety in the event of any attempt on the part of its pursuers to take it. By giving it to Tommy he would confuse the trail. The only misgiving he had was lest Tommy, who appeared to be treating the business a great deal too much in the spirit of a whimsical man joining in a round game to amuse the children, might prove an unsafe custodian.

'Buck up,' said Tommy. 'Let's have it.'

Jimmy fingered the stone undecidedly.

'You'll go showing it round to everybody.'

'I won't show it to a soul.'

'And gassing about it all over the place.'

'I won't say a word. Tombs shall be talkative compared with me. Deaf mutes shall be chatty.'

'I don't believe you half understand how important it is.'

'Of course, I do. What rot you talk. I'll guard the bally thing with my life-blood. I'll shed my last drop of gore for it. If people come looking at me through windows, I'll heave sponge-cakes at them and give them black eyes. Bless you, I know all the things one's supposed to do in a case like this. You've come to the right man. You're jolly lucky, young Jimmy Stewart, to have a chap like me about. Lots of fellows in your place would be offering me big sums to do what I'm going to do for you for nothing. So are you going to pass over that dingy pebble, or aren't you? Please yourself.'

'All right,' said Jimmy slowly. 'Here you are. But, I say, do be careful, won't you?'

'Rather. Now, observe. There's no deception. I place the object in my left trousers pocket. It is now as safe as if it were in a bank. Ask me for it back any time you like, and I'll produce it.'

'Well, mind you do,' said Jimmy.

Tommy Armstrong might have undertaken his charge less light-heartedly if he could have overheard a conversation which was going on at about the same time in a private room of a small hotel at Burlingford, a large town some twenty miles from Marleigh.

One of the speakers was the man who had sat opposite to Jimmy in the train.

The other was an Indian, a small, spare man, with dark, gleaming eyes. One of his legs was curiously twisted.

As he moved restlessly to and fro in the small room, he helped himself by means of a stick. The white man was tall and muscular, causing the other to look like a pigmy by his side; but it was noticeable that he seemed to stand in considerable awe of him.

His manner was deferential, even cringing.

'Bah!' the lame man was saying, speaking perfect English with the polished accent of the cultured Indian. 'Bah! You have made a mess of it, Marshall.'

'I assure you, sir—'

'You had *it* within your grasp. One small effort, and *it* would have been ours. In Mahomet's name, why, when this man Burrows was stricken down and helpless, did you not take *it* from him? You knew that a short search must have found *it*.'

'The alarm had been raised,' said the man who had been addressed as Marshall, with a touch of sullenness. 'The boy had run for help. Several servants were coming from the house.'

'You should have risked it. Heavens, man, is this a business where we can calculate risks? If *it* gets into Colonel Stewart's hands, we are lost. Have you any idea as to where Burrows has hidden *it*?'

'He has not hidden it.'

The brown man stopped short in his movements, and shot a keen glance at him.

'You know something?'

'I know a great deal.'

'Speak.'

'You call me a bungler—'

The brown man stamped his sound foot impatiently.

'Speak!' he repeated.

Marshall was apparently well acquainted with the tone in which he spoke the word, for he discarded without delay the somewhat aggressive manner he had assumed, and continued with the deferential air he had worn at the beginning of the interview.

'The boy, the Colonel's son, has the stone,' he said. 'I have seen it with my own eyes. I suspected that this might happen. I looked in through the window of the room where they had placed Burrows, and I saw the boy with the stone in his hand. He was returning to school today. I got into the train, and later into the same carriage. He was showing the stone to another boy. They got out at Marleigh, twenty miles down the line. They are at a school there. I saw them get out, then I came on to you.'

The brown man's eyes flashed. His body quivered with excitement.

'The task grows easier.' He muttered a few words below his breath in some strange language. 'This Burrows was a man. To deal with boys is boys' play. Marshall, you go to this Marleigh tonight.'

The first quarter of an hour after getting back to school is always a curious experience. One's friends seem strangers at first, strangers with remarkably familiar manners. The voice is the voice of Jones, and the smack on the back is the smack of Smith, but somehow we feel at first that they are not the Jones and Smith we knew last term. Then the unreal feeling passes off, and we find it hard to believe that we have not been back at school for a month instead of a quarter of an hour.

Jimmy felt particularly bewildered at first, for he plunged straight into the middle of what seemed to be a sort of indignation meeting. Everyone in the big common-room of the house – there were two houses at Marleigh, the headmaster's and Haviland's: Jimmy was in Haviland's – was talking at the same time. Nobody seemed to be doing any listening at all.

So occupied was everyone in the business of the moment that Jimmy's arrival passed unnoticed. He turned to Tommy in bewilderment.

'What's it all about?'

Tommy, putting his mouth close to Jimmy's ear, explained in a shout.

'Forgot to tell you – indignation meeting. About the food Spinder gives us.'

'What's Spinder got to do with it?'

'New housemaster. Instead of Haviland, who's ill. Don't know what's the matter with him. Scarlet fever or something. Won't be back for a good time.'

He jumped on a table.

'Chuck it, you chaps,' he yelled. 'Give us a chance. Here's Jimmy Stewart come back.' After about five minutes, having become slightly purple in the face, he managed to make himself heard. Jimmy was observed, and effusively welcomed. The interruption served to divert the meeting's attention. There was a gradual slackening of the noise, and finally comparative quiet reigned.

Then a curious-looking youth got on to the table to address the meeting. He was small, and round, and dark-skinned. He wore gold-rimmed spectacles, and a mild, benevolent expression. Cries of 'Good old Ram!' greeted him. He was evidently a popular person.

'Who's that?' asked Jimmy.

'New chap,' said Tommy. 'Comes from Calcutta. He's no end of a lark. Always trying to reform everything. He's on to this food business like a ton of bricks. Jaws nineteen to the dozen. Nobody knows his full name. It's about a mile long. It ends in Ram, so that's what he's always called. He's going to be a lawyer some day, he says. Look out. He's off!'

'Misters and fellow-sufferers,' said Ram, including all his audience in a bland wave of the hand, 'permit me to offer a few *obiter dicta*, on unhappy situation in re lamentable foodstuffs supplied to poor schoolboy by Hon'ble Spinder.'

(Cheers; and a voice, 'Good old Ram!')

'I have not long been inmate in your delightful Alma Mater, and perhaps you will say that I am a presumptuous for addressing this meeting ('No, no'). Permit me to say, misters, that we groan beneath iron-shod boots of Hon'ble Spinder. We are mere toads beneath deplorable harrow of his malignancy. (Groans). How long is this to last, misters? Are we the slaves that we should be so treated? Is Hon'ble Spinder autocratic despot that he should be allowed to oppress us? Is—'

Here he broke off on making the discovery that he had lost the attention of his audience. In default of answering the conundrums he had asked, the meeting had begun to talk again on other subjects. In one corner of the room the twins, Bob and Dick Tooth, 'the Teeth,' as they were known in the school, had started their usual fight. It was seldom that a day passed without some sort of a scuffle between them. A ring had gathered round, shouting advice and encouragement. In another corner, Binns and Sloper, the inseparables, had begun to sing a duet. It was their firm conviction that they were designed by nature for operatic stars. They sang often and loudly, and the members of their dormitory had spent hours of their valuable time in endeavouring to kick them into silence. After lights-out, when conversation had stopped and the dormitory was trying to get to sleep, one would hear a hoarse murmur from Binn's bed, 'Oi'll – er – sing thee sawongs of Arabee'; to which a hoarser murmur from Sloper's bed at the other end of the room would reply, to be a bird answering its mate, 'Ahnd ta-ales of far Cashmeerer.' Upon which the outraged occupants of the other beds would arise in their wrath, and the night would be made hideous by the thudding of pillows upon the songsters' heads.

A babel of other noises blended with these. Bellamy, the most silent boy in the school, who was reputed to be able to eat his weight, which was considerable, in any kind of food you liked to name, had retired to his locker, bored by the discussion, in which he took no interest, for food was food to Bellamy, simply that and nothing more, whatever its quality. He could have eaten cake with relish, and consequently saw nothing to complain of in the meals served to the house by Mr Spinder. He was now engaged on a particularly nerve-breaking piece of fret-sawing, which set everyone's teeth on edge. Catford and Browning were arguing hotly about a pot of jam, which Catford was alleged to have borrowed during the previous term. Catford maintained that the jam had been full and just payment for a French exercise which he had written for Browning, and that anyhow he had lent Browning a bag of biscuits during the last term but one, Browning denying both statements, and giving it as his opinion that Catford was a bloodsucker. Messrs Barr, Roberts, Halliday, and Chutwell had enlisted themselves on Browning's side, and were all talking at the same time; while Messrs Jameson, Ricketts, Coates, Harrison, and Pridbury had espoused the cause of Catford. They too, were giving their opinion of the affair all together.

Ram looked round the room pathetically, plaintively clapping his hands every now and then for silence. He might just as well have saved himself the trouble. The noise continued, unabated.

'Go it, Bob!'

'Use your left, Dick!'

'Buck up, Bob! Why don't you guard, you silly ass?'

'Dick!'

'Bob!'

'Com in-to the gar-den, Maud!'

'For the black bat-ter nah-ett hath-er-florn!'

'Com in-to the gar-den, Maud!'

'I am he-ar at ther gate alorn!'

'Well, look here, I'll take a bob for the beastly jam, if you like.'

'I've told you a dozen times—'

'Give the man his jam, Catford, you cad.'

'Don't you do it, Catford.'

'Misters, misters—!'

Jimmy looked about him, with his head buzzing. After a week of life at Marleigh he would have considered this merely ordinary, and so looked on anybody who complained of there being a good deal of noise as affected. But after the peace of holidays the strain of Marleigh conversation was a little overwhelming. He grabbed Tommy by the arm, and steered him to the door.

'What's up?' asked Tommy, in surprise, when they were outside.

'I couldn't stand that beastly row any longer.'

'Row? I didn't notice anything special. A sort of gentle murmur, perhaps.'

'Anyhow, let's go for a stroll for a bit. I say, is the food so bad?'

'It's muck,' said Tommy emphatically.

'It was all right last term.'

'I know. But then Haviland was a decent sort. Spinder's a rotter. He's sacked old Jane, and got another cook. Said Jane was not economical enough. It's a bit thick. This new woman is a perfect idiot. Can't cook for nuts. Sends everything in half raw.'

'Spinder seems to be a beast.'

'He is.'

'What sort of a looking chap is he?'

Tommy picked up a small flint from the road.

'You'd better see yourself. That,' he said, pointing to a lighted window on the ground floor, 'is his room.'

He flung the stone at the window. There was a crash of glass.

'Great Scott, man,' gasped Jimmy. 'Look out! What on earth are you playing at?'

'And that,' added Tommy calmly, as the broken window was flung up, and a head popped out, 'is Mr Spinder.'

'Who threw that stone?' shouted an angry voice.

'It's all right,' said Tommy under his breath. 'He can't possibly see us. It's much too dark. Let's be edging back to the common-room, shall we? If Spinder takes it into his head to rush out we might be caught. And then there would only be a lot of fuss. I can't stand fuss. All I ask is to be allowed to live quietly and peaceably. Come on.'

When they got back to the room, order had been restored to a certain extent. The Teeth, Robert and Richard, were cooking chestnuts together in perfect good-fellowship, reconciliation having followed war with its usual rapidity. Catford and Browning had either settled their little difference or postponed the discussion of it, and their respective gangs of followers and supporters had dispersed through the room. Somebody had taken Bellamy's fretwork away from him; and that injured youth was now sitting alone on a bench, gazing stolidly in front of him with unseeing eyes, thinking, doubtless, of the next meal. From the fact that Binns was trying to straighten his collar and smooth down his mop of ruffled hair, while Sloper's body was acting as a settee for three determined-looking boys, it seemed that the duellists had been suppressed in the usual manner.

Ram had resumed his speech, and was now well on in it.

'Masters,' he was saying, as Tommy and Jimmy entered, 'I ask you—'

'Half a second, Ram,' said Tommy. 'Sorry to interrupt, but

this is important. You shall pitch in again in a minute. I say, you chaps, do you mind each of you going out into the road for a jiffy. Come back as soon as you like. All I want you to do is to be able to say you went out.'

'What's the game, Tommy?' inquired Morrison.

From anybody but Tommy such a suggestion might have been ill received; but the red-haired one was by way of being a leader among the turbulent spirits of the house; so Morrison asked for explanation, where with anybody else he might merely have thrown a book and requested the speaker to come off it.

'It's all right. It's only that I have a sort of idea that Spinder may be in here in a minute to ask if any of us have been out in the road during the last five minutes. I don't mind telling you that *I* have. But in my modest, retiring way I don't want Spinder to know that I was the only one. See the idea?'

'Right O,' said Morrison.

There was a general movement to the door. In a few minutes everyone, with the exception of Bellamy, who still sat gazing fixedly in front of him, had gone out and come back again. The door had hardly been shut when it flew open again, to admit Mr Spinder.

The new master of the house was a small, wiry man, with a sharp face that somehow suggested some bird of prey. His nose was thin and slightly hooked, and when he was annoyed, as now, his lips closed so tightly that a thin, straight line was all that could be seen of his mouth. A pair of steely grey eyes glared from behind gold-rimmed spectacles. It was the face of a very determined man, as anybody could have seen. A student of character might have added that it was also an unscrupulous face.

Conversation died away as the master entered. Ram, who had mounted the table again with a view to resuming his speech, stood with his mouth open, looking as if he wished that he were in a less prominent position. As, indeed, he did. It was to him that Mr Spinder turned first.

'What are you doing up there?' he snapped.

'Honoured sir,' began the unfortunate orator.

'Come down at once, you buffoon.'

Ram was preparing to descend, when it occurred to him that, if he did so, the tyrant and oppressor Spinder would be left with an entirely wrong view of the case. At present it was plain that he looked upon him, Ram, not as an agitator in favour of improved food, but merely as a clown who climbed on to tables to amuse people – in fact, to do a comic turn. Ram's blood boiled at the thought. He was not, as he would have said, 'constitutionally a courageous,' but now he felt that he must speak up or forever hold his peace.

'Honoured sir,' he began again.

'Did you hear me tell you to come down from that table?'

Ram conceded this point. After all, it did not matter, so that he spoke, whether he spoke from table or floor. He climbed cautiously down with the aid of a chair.

'I came here—' said Mr Spinder.

'Honoured sir,' began Ram for the third time.

Mr Spinder fixed him with a cold stare, but the dusky orator was not to be stopped. He plunged volubly into his wrongs.

'Hon'ble Spinder,' he said, 'you are paid by parents to provide poor boys with good, wholesome food, but hoity-toity, what a falling-off is there! Our stomachs groan with beastly pangs. Listen, honourable sir, to the voice of Reason! How can brain work if body is not fed? How can poor boy floor intricacies of Latin grammar without stodgy feed? We are as if to sink with hunger. Do not think me, Hon'ble Spinder, a presumptuous for addressing you. I cannot remain hermetically sealed. The mutton,' proceeded Ram, descending to details, 'is not roasted with sufficiency. Hoity-toity and alackaday, it is of a red colour – not pleasing to look upon, and nauseous to masticate. The porridge is not an appetising. The fowl-eggs are, alackaday, frequently advancing into the sere and yellow of honourable old age. Smile indulgently, Hon'ble Spinder, on our petition. You are our father and mother and protector of the poor.'

It must not be supposed that Hon'ble Spinder had listened to this harangue with silent attention. On the contrary, he had seemed particularly restive throughout, and had made several attempts to check the orator's eloquence. Once started, however, Ram was hard to stop; and it was only when, having reached this telling appeal, he stopped to take in a little breath, that Mr Spinder found an opportunity of putting in a word. And so far from smiling indulgently, as Ram had recommended, he seemed very irritated.

'Be quiet,' he snapped. 'What is all this nonsense?'

'It's about the food, sir,' said Tommy.

'Indeed, yes, honourable sir,' put in Ram.

Mr Spinder turned on Tommy.

'What do you mean? What is wrong with the food?'

'It's beastly,' said a voice.

Mr Spinder wheeled round.

'Who said that?'

No reply.

'The boy who made that remark step forward.'

There was no response to this invitation. Mr Spinder stood for a moment, frowning, then turned to Tommy again.

'What is wrong with the food, Armstrong?'

'It's so badly cooked, sir,' said Tommy.

'What!'

'It's hardly cooked at all sometimes. Couldn't we have old Jane back again instead of this new cook, sir?'

'When I require advice from you, Armstrong,' said Mr Spinder, 'on the subject of the management of this house, I will ask for it.'

'Yes, sir.'

'The cooking is perfectly satisfactory. Boys nowadays expect to be pampered.'

'No, sir.'

'What do you mean, Armstrong?'

'They don't expect to be pampered, sir. They only expect to get something except raw meat.'

Mr Spinder's mouth tightened.

'You will do me a hundred lines, Armstrong, for impertinence.'

'Yes, sir.'

'Hoity-toity, honourable sir,' began Ram excitedly.

'Be quiet,' snapped the master, turning on him like a flash. Ram subsided as if he had been suddenly punctured. Mr Spinder took advantage of the silence to drop the food subject, and turn to the matter which had originally brought him to the room.

'I came here,' he said, 'to ask if any of you boys had been out in the road during the last quarter of an hour?'

'Yes, sir,' said Jimmy, speaking for the first time.

'Ah! Who are you?'

'Stewart, sir. I only came back today.'

'Oh, yes. The boy who had mumps. Were you out in the road just now?'

'Yes, sir. We all were.'

'You all were? Why?'

'We thought we heard a crash of glass, sir.'

Tommy looked admiringly at Jimmy. This was genius.

Mr Spinder was surprised. He had taken it for granted that his window had been broken by one of the boys in his house; but this seemed to suggest that some outside person had done the thing.

'Did you all go out together?' he asked.

'Yes, sir,' said half a dozen voices.

'H'm.' Mr Spinder walked to the door.

Arriving there, he turned.

'From what I have heard tonight,' he said, 'I gather that there is a great deal of foolish agitation going on. Some of you, I know, can only be looked on and treated as children' – here he motioned towards the unhappy Ram, who blinked pathetically at him through his glasses – 'but you others, I should imagine, are sufficiently sensible to understand what is said to you. I say, once and for all, that I will not have any more of this nonsense about the food. The food is perfectly good. The cooking is quite satisfactory. I will not have any of this hole-in-the-corner business of grumbling among yourselves in corners. Do you all understand me? I hope I shall not have to speak of this again.'

He turned on his heel, and left the room.

There was silence for a moment after he had gone. It was broken by Ram.

'Misters and fellow-students,' he cried, 'is this to be borne? Are we the slaves? We must act, sirs, we must act.'

'You needn't act the goat, anyhow,' said Morrison unkindly. 'What's to be done, Tommy?'

'My hundred lines, as a start, dash it,' said Tommy. 'After that I'll devote my powerful brain to the matter. We must think of something.'

'Pretty quick, too,' said Morrison, 'or we shall all be poisoned.'

Tommy Armstrong's was one of those great minds which become restless unless fully employed. It was a source of much inconvenience to him that the ordinary affairs of school life did not employ it fully, which led to his being frequently compelled to spend hours, when he might have been doing something more pleasant, in working off commissions in the shape of lines and other impositions. This term it looked as if life out of school might be a little more interesting than usual. Tommy had a good deal of Irish blood in his veins, and he loved a row. The feeling in the house about the food, and Mr Spinder's truculent attitude, made it seem likely that there would be several rows that term. Altogether, as far as out-of-school hours were concerned, he was very fairly satisfied with things. But his active mind still needed employment in the class-room. And this was especially the case during the German lesson, presided over by Herr Steingruber.

The German master was a man of wide learning – he had taken degrees at Heidelberg University, and was the author of more than one book on the grammar and construction of his native language – but he did not infuse excitement into a lesson. It was Tommy's habit, therefore, to do this for him.

On the present occasion the first half of the lesson was allowed to pass quietly, as far as he was concerned. The hundred lines which Mr Spinder had given him on the previous evening had to be worked off; and Tommy spent half an hour writing them behind the cover of a pile of books. Herr Steingruber's studies at Heidelberg University, where he had burnt the midnight oil with great regularity and perseverance, had improved his brain but weakened his sight. He was now extremely short-sighted, and even with the aid of a huge pair of glasses could not see any great distance.

Tommy, who sat at one side of the room, out of the direct range of vision, was therefore quite safe. He wrote on, while the Herr lectured ponderously on German verbs, until the hundred lines were completed. Then, with the satisfying feeling that his duty had been done, he blotted the last page, and began to look about him in search of some employment to amuse him during the remaining half-hour of the lesson.

An idea occurred to him almost at once. Herr Steingruber, in his lecture on German verbs, had now reached the stage where it was necessary for him to perform with chalk on the blackboard. A rather tricky relationship between two families of verbs had to be illustrated and explained. His method of procedure was to draw a sort of chart on the blackboard, and then to turn his back and go further into the matter verbally.

This struck Tommy as a chance which it would be rash to miss. He took a golf-ball from his pocket. There were some links near the school, where the masters were in the habit of playing. Tommy had found the ball in some gorse bushes during a Sunday ramble on the links.

'If,' said Herr Steingruber, 'we would of idiomatig Sherman masters begom, we must remember' – he turned to the blackboard, drew a few strokes with the chalk, wrote in a couple of words, and turned away again – 'zo!'

As he turned Tommy flung his golf-ball at the board, caught it as it rebounded, and, by the time the Herr had turned round, had replaced it in his pocket. The noise made by the ball striking the board was like the crack of a rifle. Herr Steingruber leaped quite a foot into the air.

'Ach Himmel,' he cried, 'vhat vos dot?'

Explanations came from all corners of the room.

'Thunder, I think, sir,' said Binns.

'Somebody shooting with a rifle outside, sir,' said Sloper.

Catford thought it might have been somebody's braces bursting.

Browning stated that he would not be surprised if it wasn't the start-off of an earth-quake.

'I believe it was the blackboard, sir,' said Tommy respectfully. 'It might be a flaw in the wood, sir, which made it go crack like that.'

'Ach, vell,' said Herr Steingruber, philosophically, 'more dings in heaven and earth dere are, as your boet Shakesbeare says. De condemblation of de Sherman verbs resume let us, my liddle students. I vill a zendence write in idiomatig Sherman, which of these two verbs the peguliarities illusdrates. Zo.'

He wrote the idiomatic sentence, and turned away from the board.

'Of dot zendence der meaning vos, "Gretchen, der frau – der wife of der miller—"'

Crack!

The German master's remarks on Gretchen, the wife of the miller, were cut short. He stared, deeply perplexed, at the blackboard.

'I'm certain it's thunder, sir,' said Binns. 'There's going to be an awful storm.'

'It's a rifle, sir, I'm sure,' said Sloper.

'It must be something in the wood the blackboard's made of, sir,' said Tommy. 'It's probably got too dry or something. I believe wood often cracks like that when it gets dry.'

'Zilence, zilence,' said Herr Steingruber. 'Too moch chadder und exblanation-talk there is. Led us now the verbs und their so interesding peculiarities for a moment leave, und to our dranslation durn. Oben, my liddle men, at bage vorty-seven your dranslation books. Zloper, begin. I vill der English virst read, und den you vill into idiomatig Sherman id dranslate. Zilence, blease, all, vhile I virst der English glearly read. "In der garden of my ungle's vriend zere are roses, gabbages, bees, und abbles. Der liddle dog, Hans, vrisks in der bushes. My ungle's vriend's zister is on the lawn zeated." Zo. Now, Zloper.'

Sloper's translation of this passage was so faulty that the calm of the lesson was little by little disturbed till Herr Steingruber, in spite of his philosophy, was plucking at his moustache, and passing his fingers in an agitated manner through his hair.

'Ach, Himmel, my liddle Zloper,' he cried, in a sort of agony. 'Bad, wrong id is. Nod idiomatig id is. Again der last bassage dranslate.'

'My liddle Zloper,' with an injured air, as if he preferred his own version, but gave in to oblige Herr Steingruber, was proceeding to take the passage again, when he paused, and gazed at the German master, surprised at the latter's singular behaviour. The Herr was bending down, and apparently peering at an object on the floor. Those nearest could see that it was a sixpence. The Herr saw this. What he did not see was that it had a hole in it, and was attached to a very thin thread of silk, the other end of which was firmly grasped in Tommy Armstrong's hand.

Bending down, the German master made a grab at the coin.

To his surprise, he found that he had misjudged the distance. His hand struck the floor quite a foot away from the coin.

He rose, and polished his glasses. The excitement in the room was now great. Everyone was bending forward from his seat, to watch better the movements of the treasurer-hunter. Every face expressed sympathetic interest.

The German master stooped down, and made another grab. Again he found that he had miscalculated the distance. The coin remained on the floor.

Again he rose, and polished his glasses. Then, this operation concluded, he prepared to make a third assault, determined that this time there should be no mistake. When he looked at the floor the sixpence was gone.

He peered round suspiciously through his glasses.

'Who has der zixpence daken? Binns, haf you der zixpence daken?'

'Sixpence, sir? What sixpence?'

'Der zixpence dat on der floor vas.'

'Sixpence on the floor, sir? Where, sir?'

'It is gon. But on der floor id vos.'

'Was that what you were trying to get hold of, sir? I thought you were catching butterflies.'

'Voolish boy, dere vos no butterflies in der winter. It vos a zixpence dat on her floor vos.'

'*I* haven't taken—'

Crack!

Herr Steingruber spun round. There was the blackboard, looking just the same as usual. He went up to it, and examined it closely. Nothing seemed to be wrong with it.

'It's bad wood, sir,' said Tommy. 'That's what it is. You ought to get rid of it at once, sir.'

'Zilence! Of dis exblanation-chadder dere always doo moch is. Zloper, broceed with der idiomatig Sherman dranslation.'

The German master returned to his seat, thoroughly disturbed. The episode of the vanishing sixpence had worried him. He was perfectly certain that there had been a sixpence there. But how could a sixpence have moved of its own accord? Herr Steingruber felt suspicious. There was more in this than met the eye. He was on the alert. As Sloper blundered through the passage about the little dog, Hans, and the uncle's friend's sister, the German master's senses were unusually active.

It was this that enabled him to see that Tommy Armstrong was not attending to the lesson, but examining something under the desk.

He crouched like a tiger. Tommy's attention was fixed on what he held in his hand.

Herr Steingruber sprang. He was at Tommy's side before the latter knew what was happening.

'Give me dat, Armstrong. Zo! you der hours of lesson waste in with foolish doys blaying? Zo! I vill id gonfisgate.'

'Id' was Jimmy's precious blue stone. Tommy had taken it out to look at it.

Herr Steingruber placed it in his pocket, and walked back to his seat.

Tommy was not one of those over-sensitive people who shrink from any situation which is likely to be at all unpleasant. Rather the reverse, in fact. Situations which might have seemed unpleasant to the ordinary person did not disturb Tommy at all. When in the previous term, shooting with a catapult, he had put a bullet, purely by accident, through a stout gentleman's top-hat, Tommy had apologised with an easy grace which suggested that the thing struck him merely as an amusing joke against himself. When he had been caught in the very act of lighting a Chinese cracker during a French lesson, he had not turned a hair.

But now he did shrink, to a certain extent, from the task of explaining to Jimmy that the stone entrusted to his care was at that moment lying in Herr Steingruber's capacious waistcoat-pocket. Jimmy had seemed to set such store on that dingy pebble. Tommy was conscious of feeling a little uncertain as to how he would take the story of its loss.

He broke the bad news to him after school.

By way of breaking it gently he led off with a repetition of his favourite remark, that he didn't think much of the stone. 'It's a rotten sort of thing,' he said. 'No good to anybody, really. You aren't really awfully keen on it, are you?'

'Great Scott,' cried Jimmy. 'You haven't lost it?'

'Lost it! Good heavens, no. Do you think I can't look after a thing?'

'Sorry. I thought from what you said—'

'Oh, no. I haven't lost it. The fact is—'

'Well?'

'Well, it was like this. I had got frightfully nervous about it, wanting to see that it was safe and all that, and I just took it out of my pocket, to look at, just to see that it was all right, you know, and – well, it somehow happened that old Steingruber was hanging about, and – well, he collared it. It's nothing to look so cut up about,' he added, catching sight of Jimmy's face. 'I'll get it back all right. I tried to after school. I went up to him, and asked him to play the 'cello to me this afternoon, but he wasn't taking any. The fact is, we were ragging a good bit in form today, and he was a bit fed up.'

'It's my fault,' said Jimmy resignedly. 'I ought never to have let the thing out of my hands. It can't be helped now, though.'

'That's right. Keep looking on the bright side.'

'I'll go and see old Steingruber about it after school. He'll probably be feeling better then. Anyhow, when I tell him the thing's really mine, he'll let me have it back, I should think.'

'Certain to. He's a good old sort.'

Jimmy found it difficult to keep his mind on his work that afternoon. The loss of the blue stone worried him. It was not quite so bad as if it had actually been lost, of course. Herr Steingruber might be relied upon to keep it safe; and, if approached properly when in his usual good temper, would almost certainly give it back. The German master was fond of the boys, and his wrath never lasted long. But, nevertheless, Jimmy was worried. One result of which was that he received one hundred lines from Mr Spinder for inattention.

He resolved to approach Herr Steingruber at once.

When he came to the latter's room, however, he found that he was not there. Herr Steingruber, he was informed, had gone out to the links to play golf with Mr Spinder. Jimmy decided to postpone his appeal till his return.

The Herr, meanwhile, with his bag of clubs under his arm, was trudging round the links with Mr Spinder. The latter was a good golfer, but the Herr, at present, was a novice. He was vigorous and enthusiastic, but he lacked skill.

They were now at the fourth tee. Mr Spinder drove off, a hard, skimming drive which took him on to the green. Then Herr Steingruber stepped forward.

It was a pleasant sight to see the German master at work on the links. He had a way of addressing the ball that was all his own. He stood with legs widely stretched, a fixed and serious expression on his face. Swaying slightly, he waggled his club to and fro for a few moments, then very slowly raised it above his shoulder. Then, drawing a deep breath, he swiped. The ball remained where it was. Breathing a guttural exclamation, he proceeded, still with the same fixed look, to get into position again. This time about a foot of turf came away, gashed up by his club. Herr Steingruber looked at it owlishly.

'How happen did dot?' he asked.

'You did not keep your eye on the ball,' said Mr Spinder.

'Ach, Himmel, my eye on der ball from der very beginning vos. Vhot shall I now do?'

'Better replace England first of all,' suggested his opponent. The Herr picked up the slab of turf, and patted it down into its place. After which he got into position again.

This time he was more fortunate. By a singular accident he happened to strike the ball full and fair. There was always plenty of power in his strokes, so that when, as now, he managed to hit the ball, it always travelled. On this occasion, aided by a puff of wind, it hummed through the air, and landed on the green, only a yard behind his opponent's.

'Zo!' he grunted triumphantly.

With the luck of the beginner at golf he continued his success. His first putt sent the ball into the hole.

'Zo! I imbrove!' he said.

Mr Spinder, muttering something under his breath about flukes, turned to his own ball. Putting was his weak point, and it took him two more strokes to hole out. As he was giving his opponent two strokes a hole, this meant that he had not managed even to halve the hole with him. The German master was puffed up with honest pride as they made their way to the next tee.

The fifth hole also fell to Herr Steingruber. He plodded along, and did it in eight. Mr Spinder, getting entangled in a bunker, which the Herr had miraculously contrived to avoid, could only hole out in seven.

By this time the Herr was jubilant. His opponent, who never liked being beaten, even when he was giving away strokes, was silent and gloomy. The Herr, beaming, began to enlarge on the situation.

'Almost I begin to dthink,' he said, 'dot it vos my liddle masgot dot makes me today so well blay. Yah, dot vos der liddle shap.'

'I don't know what you're talking about, Steingruber; but I am waiting for you to drive off.'

'Drive off will I, but virst my liddle masgot most I douch.'

He thrust a finger into his waistcoat-pocket.

'I should like to see this mascot,' said Mr Spinder. 'It must be a remarkably powerful charm if it gives you the sort of luck you have been having during this round. A remarkably powerful charm.'

'Dis vos him.'

Herr Steingruber extended the blue stone towards his opponent between a gigantic thumb and forefinger. Mr Spinder took it.

As he looked at it, a close observer might have noticed him start. He gazed at the small object on the palm of his hand with as keen an interest as if it had been the Koh-i-noor. Herr Steingruber prattled on.

'It vos during der lesson doday. I see der boy Armsdrong with zomeding under der desk blaying. I do myself "Zo!" zay. "What is id dot der liddle Armsdrong do zo with inderest und addention examine?" Der boy gontinue do examine what he do examine. But me I do wait my obbordunity. I grouch. I sbring. "What is id, boy," I say, "that you instead of addending do your Sherman dranslation loog ad?" Id vos dis liddle masgot. I id convisgate. Und id bring me der goot lug ad der golf-game. Zo.'

Mr Spinder continued to behave, as, according to the Herr, Tommy Armstrong had done. His whole attention seemed wrapped up in the blue stone.

'How did you get it?' he said, in a voice which, though the German master did not notice it, was tremulous with excitement.

'I vos telling you, my Sbinder. From der boy Armstrong in der glass-room. He vos with id blaying, when I grouch, I sbring, und I id gonfisgate.'

'But how did it come into his possession?'

'Zot I do not know.'

Mr Spinder, with a deep breath, handed back the stone, which the German master replaced in his waistcoat-pocket.

'Do my heart next,' he explained humorously.

'Shall we go on with the game?' said Mr Spinder.

The Herr prepared once more to address the ball. This time the mascot seemed to have lost its power temporarily. A sandy bunker lay between the tee and the hole. Into this his ball flew. His face clouded, but cleared again almost immediately, for his opponent's ball performed exactly the same manoeuvre.

'We are in misfortune gombanions, my Sbinder,' he remarked.

At the bunker he drew out the stone again. Then, replacing it, he succeeded, after three attempts, in getting his ball to the other side.

'Let me have another look at that stone, Steingruber,' said Mr Spinder. 'It interests me.' He took it in his hand, but hardly had he done so when he let it fall into the sand. Stooping quickly, he had picked it up and transferred it to his own pocket before the short-sighted German master could see what was happening.

'I am extremely sorry, Steingruber,' he said. 'I have dropped your mascot into the sand. Don't you bother. I will look for it.' But, after a prolonged search, he rose to his feet empty-handed.

'I fear it is lost,' he said. 'This sand makes it impossible to find a small object like that. I am extremely sorry. It was inexcusably careless of me.'

'My masgot,' moaned the German master.

'Never mind,' said Mr Spinder. 'When a golfer loses his opponent's mascot, he is far more likely to bring bad luck to himself than to his opponent. Let us play on, shall we?'

And it seemed as if he were right in his supposition, for, though Herr Steingruber played badly, Mr Spinder played worse; and at the conclusion of the round the German master had won a substantial victory, and was thoroughly pleased with life once more.

Directly he heard that the golfers had been seen on the school premises, Jimmy hurried to Herr Steingruber's room, to open negotiations respecting the blue stone. He found the Herr standing in the middle of the floor, addressing an imaginary ball with a brassy. The table was pushed back against the wall, the chairs were stacked in a heap in one corner of the room, and there were some pieces of broken china on the carpet, for Herr Steingruber, in his efforts to improve his game, had broken a gas-globe.

The German master opened conversation directly Jimmy entered.

'All der gread masders of der game,' he said, 'der indoor for imbroving der swing bractice regommend. Der feet well abart und virmly vixed do der ground, der zlow zwing up mit der eyes vixed always on der ball; und der quick zwing down—'

Here he suited the action to the words, and the 'quick zwing down' nearly took Jimmy on the shin. He jumped back. Herr Steingruber was full of apologies.

'Ach, zo! Vorgetting was I dot der sbace in dis room gonfined vos. Almost I give you der nasty sore blace, my liddle Zdewart. Dot vos voolishness of me, zo?'

'It's all right, sir,' said Jimmy. 'No harm done. Shall I pick up this broken china?'

The German master looked blankly at the ruins on the floor.

'Ach Himmel, how I dot done? Dot der Braid lofding-shot must have been. I vos der gareless shap, hein? Jah, my liddle vellow, der bieces pick up. I must my indoor-bractice do der bood-room gonfine. Zo.'

Jimmy picked up the broken globe, put the pieces in the fire-place, and turned to business.

'Please, sir, do you remember taking a queer little blue stone from Armstrong this morning?'

'Jah! Dot my masgot vos. Der liddle Armsdrong with id in der Sherman lesson play, und I grouch, I sbring, und I id con-fisgate. Zo.'

'I was wondering if you would let me have it back, sir. It was mine, really. I only lent it to Armstrong. I should be awfully obliged if you would give it me, sir. I promised the man who gave it me that I would take great care of it. He'd be sick—'

'Zick? How dot vos?'

'Annoyed, sir. He'd be very much annoyed if I hadn't got it when he asked me for it.'

The soft-hearted German master was touched.

'Ach, my liddle Zdewart, vot you gall kettle of fish dis vos. As your boet says, of all zad vorts of dongue or ben, der zaddest vos dese, it mide haf been. Willingly would I der ztone redurn, had I id; but, alas! on der lingks dis afternoon Mr Sbinder he says, "Let me at dot liddle sdone loog," und I id to him give, und he id in der sand of der bunker garelessly drops. Id is lost, my liddle vellow, dis blay-thing of yours.'

'Lost, sir!'

Jimmy's voice showed his dismay. The good-natured German master was sorry for him.

'Ach, do not zorrowful be, my liddle Zdewart. Zis zo disdressing agcident you vill in dime vorget. See! Here is a shillung. Zpend it on zweets, und vorget der lost blay-thing.'

Jimmy declined the proffered coin.

'It's all right, sir,' he said. 'It really doesn't matter. If it's lost, it can't be helped.'

Herr Steingruber beamed approvingly. 'Dot vos der vilosophigal sbirit, Zdewart, vich I vos glad do zee. In Shermany we are all vilosophers. We do not shed der tear. We zay, as you have zaid, "All right!" Dot vos der broper sdate of mind, Zdewart. Jah, zo.'

Jimmy retired, feeling in anything but that philosophical frame of mind which Herr Steingruber had praised so highly. What he was to say to Sam Burrows when he came and asked for the stone he did not like to think. Nor could he imagine what the consequences of the loss might be. Sam had hinted vaguely at tremendous issues that hung on the blue stone. He felt more than ever that he had been a fool to entrust so valuable a piece of property to a reckless fellow like Tommy. He was enough of a philosopher not to feel too sore against the latter. He realised that it was really all his own fault. It was not as if he had not known what sort of a fellow Tommy was. Knowing him to be careless and casual, he ought never to have let him have the stone at all.

He was feeling very sorry for himself as he went back to the common-room to write the hundred lines which Mr Spinder had set him to do.

Mr Spinder, meanwhile, was also busily occupied. Seated in his room at a table, lit by a green-shaded lamp, he was poring over a ponderous volume of Indian history. The boys at Marleigh knew nothing of it, but Mr Spinder had almost a European reputation as an authority on the more obscure by-ways of Indian life and thought. He had taken the study up at Oxford more as a hobby than anything else, and it had fascinated him. There were probably not three men in the country who knew more than Mr Spinder about the curious thoughts and superstitions of the Indian.

His whole body was quivering with excitement as he read. He passed his fingers nervously through his thin hair.

'It is,' he murmured. 'It must be. The description tallies exactly. "Now this stone is called the Tear of Heaven, for it is blue as the skies and misty as a tear. And on it are the words written, *Allah is God.*" The Tear of Heaven! The Sacred Stone itself! What miracle brought it here? What does it all mean?'

He took out the blue stone, and gazed at it fixedly in the lamplight.

'"Blue as the skies and misty as a tear." It is. It must be. What stupendous good fortune. "Allah is God."'

He rose from his seat, and strode to and fro nervously. His hands trembled as he walked. The pupils of his eyes had narrowed to pin-points.

As he stood by the table, looking down at the blue stone, there was a knock at the door. He was too engrossed to hear it. The knock was repeated. Still he paid no attention.

The door opened, and Jimmy walked in, bearing some sheets of foolscap.

Jimmy had managed to finish his hundred lines in record time. Tommy Armstrong, always full of ingenious schemes, had hit upon a labour-saving device, not unconnected with the tying together of three penholders. This had enabled Jimmy to get through his imposition with unparalleled speed.

Not getting any answer to his knocks, he had walked into the room, to find Mr Spinder apparently absorbed in contemplation of some object on the table. Jimmy went towards him, his footsteps making little noise on the soft carpet. And as he got to the table, he saw what it was that was occupying the master's attention. There on the table, in the full glare of the lamp, was the lost stone.

Jimmy was unable to repress a slight cry of astonishment. Mr Spinder turned like a trapped animal, his face blazing with anger. 'Who are you? What do you want?' With a swift movement of his hand he seized the stone, and put it in his pocket. 'Why did you come in without knocking?'

'I did knock, sir,' said Jimmy. 'But you didn't hear me. I knocked twice. I came to show up my lines.'

'Put them down, put them down. Thank you, that will do; you may go.'

'May I have that stone, sir?' said Jimmy. 'It was really mine, only I lent it to Armstrong, and Herr Steingruber confiscated it. Can I have it back?'

Mr Spinder was calm again now, icily calm.

He looked at Jimmy through his spectacles.

'Let me see, your name is Stewart, isn't it? Ah, yes. What were you saying, Stewart?'

'I asked if I might have back that blue stone, sir.'

'You seem to be labouring under some curious delusion, Stewart. What stone is this you are speaking of?'

'The stone you put in your pocket just now, sir.'

Mr Spinder's eyebrows went up.

'I still fail to understand what you are talking about, Stewart. I put no stone in my pocket.'

'I saw you, sir.'

'Really, Stewart! It is a little unusual, is it not, for a boy to disbelieve a master's word? I am afraid you will be getting yourself into trouble if you do not break yourself of that habit. I assure you I know nothing of this stone you mention. Why should I? From your own account it seems that Herr Steingruber should know more about it than I. You may go, Stewart. I take it that you do not propose to search me? That will do, then. Close the door behind you.'

Jimmy was helpless. He realised that. He was as certain as he had ever been of anything that he had seen Mr Spinder place the blue stone in his pocket; but he knew that he had no means of proving it. Mr Spinder could bring Herr Steingruber to witness that the stone had been lost on the golf-links. Jimmy saw that, at any rate, for the time, he was beaten. He left the room without another word.

The mystery of the thing began to bewilder him more and more. What was this blue stone that Mr Spinder should deliberately steal it, and then lie to hide the fact that he had stolen it? The stone had evidently a value which the ordinary person did not recognise. Witness the attitude of Tommy Armstrong and Herr Steingruber towards it. Why should Mr Spinder of all people recognise this value? Jimmy worried over these problems till he went to bed, and far into the night.

Next day there were distractions. During breakfast Tommy Armstrong, by way of drawing attention to the inferior state of the food supplied to the house, had taken the step of letting loose a live chicken, which he had bought for the purpose on the previous afternoon, and preserved during the night in a cardboard box with holes bored in the lid. The bird, surprised and relieved to find itself once more at liberty, had sprinted joyfully down the table in Mr Spinder's direction, finally tripping over his plate, and falling on to his waistcoat as if Mr Spinder were

his long-lost brother. Mr Spinder rose, white with rage. 'Who brought that bird into the room?' he cried.

There was a moment's silence. After which Tommy said that he thought it must have come out of one of the eggs. A raucous laugh, in unison, from the Teeth brothers, had brought Mr Spinder's wrath to the boiling-point. He stammered in his fury.

Just as it seemed that he might proceed to attack Tommy, and engage him in a hand-to-hand struggle, his attention was diverted by the chicken, which, after lying on the floor for a while in an apparently fainting condition, now revived, and made a dash for the door. Everybody rose from his place, and charged after it, with the exception of Bellamy, who continued to pound away steadily at bread-and-butter. In the confusion Mr Spinder forgot Tommy; and when things were comparatively quiet again, he informed the whole house that it would write him out the first ten pages of the Latin grammar. He then swept out of the room, followed by the chicken, which had once more got loose. The first skirmish, it was felt, had ended rather in his favour. The general opinion of the house was that further steps would have to be taken. The thing was discussed in the common-room after school.

'It's no good doing things on a small scale like this,' said Tommy. 'He's bound to score. He just sets us imposts, and there we are. What we want is to organise. We must have a regular strike. For goodness' sake, somebody, kill those two farmyard-imitators.'

This remark was caused by the thoughtless behaviour of Binns and Sloper, who, not finding the debate greatly to their interest, had begun to sing an extract from the music-hall songs of the day. Sloper had just requested some person unknown to put him amongst the girls, to which Binns had added explanatorily, anxious apparently that there should be no mistake, 'those with the curly curls,' when the meeting descended upon the warblers in the usual manner, and the duet came to an end in a cloud of dust.

'Forge ahead, Tommy,' said Catford, from his seat on Binns' chest. 'You were saying something about striking.'

'Yes. I've got an idea. Suppose we all absolutely refused to touch the food. He couldn't do anything then. There's no rule forcing one to eat. We would be quite quiet and respectful about it, only we would simply not touch the stuff. He'd have to do something then. What do you think about it?'

It seemed that the meeting thought a good deal about it, one way and another. A perfect babel of sound arose, everybody giving his opinion as loud as he was able. The plump form of Ram was seen placidly climbing on to his favourite table. Ram was the popular orator, and his appearance was nearly always the signal for silence.

'Hon'ble Armstrong,' said Ram, 'must forgive me if I meet his suggestion with a *nolo episcopari* and miss-in-baulk. For why, misters? Hon'ble Armstrong has asked us to abstain from food and to let no mutton, no beef, no fowl egg pass the locked door of our firmly-clenched teeth. But, lackaday, this is surely as if to milk the ram. For how without food, even if that food be the unappetising and a bit off, shall we support life and not pop off mortal coil, as Hon'ble Shakespeare says? 'Tis better, misters, as Hon'ble Shakespeare also says, to bear with the ship-snaps we know of than fly to others which may prove but a jumping from frying-pan into fire. Half a loaf is better than an entire nullity of the staff of life. Hoity-toity, without food we shall as if to swoon away on class-room floor.'

These eminently sound opinions were greeted with applause. Tommy, however, did not seem to think much of them.

'You silly goat,' he said, complainingly, 'I never meant that we should do the fasting man act. If you thought more and jawed less, Ram, you'd get on better.'

'What *is* the idea?' asked Browning.

'Why, simply to lay in a stock of grub on our own. Chaps in

the Army often do it. If they get fed up with the grub that's served out to them, they just sit tight and wait till afterwards, when they have a chance of buying what they want. See the idea? Let's lay in supplies, and then we can begin to get moving.'

'It's not a bad idea,' said Morrison. 'But where's the money to come from?'

'*Rem acu tetigisti*,' said Ram. 'You have touched the spot, Hon'ble Morrison. Where are we to find the sinews of war?'

'We'd better have a whip round,' said Tommy. 'I'll lead off with a quid. My uncle gave me one when I went to see him.'

The magnificence of this offer impressed the meeting. Here was something practical. Now he *was* talking. Unfortunately, the other donations fell a good deal short of this lofty standard. The Teeth happened to have had a postal order for five shillings by that morning's post from an indulgent grandmother; and Catford disgorged half a crown, but the sum total of the collection only panned out at two pounds. A penny less, to be exact.

'The question is,' said Tommy, having counted the money, 'how long can we keep going on two quid? There are thirty of us here. That only works out at a bit over a bob each. You can't go on long on a bob and two-pence, or whatever it is.'

A blank gloom settled on the meeting. Two pounds had seemed an enormous sum up till then, but, looked at in that way, as having to be divided up amongst thirty boys, there did not appear to be so much of it as one thought.

Tommy was the first to recover from the shock.

'I tell you what it is,' he said. 'We must raise some more. For the strike to be worth anything we must be ready to go on with it for nearly a week. It's no good doing it for one day. He'd simply think we'd got the pip or something. Everyone had better write home for money. If that fails, we shall have to try something else.'

A muffled voice spoke from the floor. It was recognised as that of Sloper.

'If one or two of you men of wrath would kindly get off my chest,' said the voice, 'I should like to make a suggestion. Don't mind me, though: I don't want to spoil your simple pleasures.'

'Let him up,' said Tommy. 'But if you only want to break into one of your beastly songs again, you'll jolly well be knocked down and jumped on by the whole strength of the company.'

'You wrong me,' said Sloper. 'You pain me deeply. All I wanted was to do you a good turn. It's like this. Why not give a concert in aid of the strike fund, and charge sixpence or a bob for admission? Binns and I,' added the speaker, modestly, 'wouldn't mind giving you the benefit of our trained skill. We'll sing as many songs as you like.'

'I bet you will,' said Tommy. 'It's not a bad idea, though, I must say. The fellows would roll up like anything, especially if we told them what it was for.'

'We could hold it in the gym,' suggested Binns. 'Sloper and I would do a duet we heard in the pantomime last year. It goes like this.'

But the audience were on the watch, and headed him off.

'Chuck it,' said Tommy. 'Plenty of time for that. No need to hear your beastly voice before the night. What do you chaps say to this concert idea?'

Everybody seemed in favour of it. There was more talent in Spinder's house common-room, it appeared, than the casual observer would have imagined. The place simply reeked with it. Ram offered to recite Shakespeare. The only difficulty with Binns and Sloper was to prevent them monopolising the entire bill. Catford thought he could remember some conjuring tricks, if given time. The Teeth volunteered to box a few rounds. And nearly everybody else had something to offer.

'Good,' said Tommy. 'It's going to be a strong programme. Hullo, Morrison, what are you going to do? Play any instrument? Or is a song more in your line?'

'I don't know what you're jawing about,' said Morrison, who had just entered. 'Is Jimmy Stewart anywhere about? Oh, there you are, Jimmy. I say, I met a man out in the road who says he wants to see you. Wouldn't tell me what it was about. So I said I'd nip in and fetch you. He looks like an old soldier. Says his name's Burrows. Got one arm in a sling.'

'Where is he?' asked Jimmy dismally. Sam Burrows was the last man in the world he wanted to see just then.

A dim figure loomed up in the darkness as Jimmy went out into the road.

'That you, matey?' said a voice.

'Hullo,' said Jimmy.

The figure drew a deep breath, and came a step nearer. It was Sam Burrows, sure enough. Jimmy saw that, as Morrison had said, his arm was in a sling. His first question concerned itself with Sam's wound.

'How's your shoulder?' he asked. 'Surely it can't be all right again yet?'

'Rightly speaking, sir, it isn't. I expect the doctor is sayin' things about me at this very moment. "Don't you dream of stirring for a week," he says. "Right, sir," says I. But, love us, I couldn't keep lying on my back, wondering all the while if that brawsted blackie with the twisted leg had got hold of the stone, and if you'd been shot at same as me. I couldn't do it, matey. Thinking of it over, as I lay there, I says to myself, "Sam, you've been and played that young gentleman a dirty trick. What d'you mean by shifting all the responserbility off of your own shoulders on to his?" And I says, "You just go off quietly, without saying a word to the doctor, and get that stone back from him, and see the thing through off yer own. It ain't fair to a nipper to put such a thing on to him." So last night I slips out of the house, treks quietly to the station, and waits for the first train. And here I am, so now let's have that bit of blue ruin back, matey, and you can go and sleep quietly in your little bed, which I lay you haven't done up to now. Let's have it, matey.'

Jimmy did not attempt to break the thing gently.

'I can't,' he said miserably. 'It's gone.'

Sam stood stock still for a second before speaking.

'Gawd!' he said at last. 'What!'

'It's gone.'

'Gone! 'Ow? They ain't bin and got it? Not that blackie and his gang?'

'No, it's not him. It's not been stolen at all, really.'

'You ain't lost it?'

Jimmy explained. Sam listened attentively. When Jimmy had come to the end of his story, he whistled.

'It's a rum start,' he said. 'This 'ere What's-his-name, now—'

'Spinder.'

'This 'ere Spinder. What's his game?'

'I can't make out. That's what's puzzling me. I'm as certain as anything that I saw him take the stone off the table and shove it into his pocket. I know he was lying when he said he hadn't. I couldn't do anything, of course. But he's got it, I know.'

'What sort of a man might he be?'

'I don't know. He's a new master. He only came this term. Nobody seems to like him much. But I don't know why he should take the stone.'

'But he has?'

'I'm absolutely certain of it.'

'And you ain't seen anything of the blackie and his lot?'

'Not since I got here. But – I didn't tell you at the time—'

'What's that, matey?'

Jimmy related briefly all that had taken place on the night of Sam's injury, and the day after – the face at the window, the burglar, the man in the train, and the unfortunate request of Tommy Armstrong to be shown the blue stone. Sam sucked in his breath. He was plainly deeply interested.

'This 'ere chum of yours, Tommy What's-'is-name, seems to be one of the cloth-heads, he does. Pity he ain't got more sense in him.'

'He's rather mucked things up, hasn't he? But, of course, he didn't realise how awfully important the stone was.'

'He's put the lid on it, he has,' said Sam. ''E's brought the whole gang of them on your track, and now he's let this 'ere Spinder get 'old of the stone. The only thing to be done now is to try and get it back from Spinder. That's what we must do.'

'But how?'

'Ah, that's it. How? Where does he live, now?'

'That's his window over there on the ground floor.'

'On the ground floor,' repeated Sam thoughtfully. 'That window with the red blind, I take it.'

'That's the one.'

'I see. Well, the only thing now is to sit and think things over a bit. Let's only 'ope as how it's only this Mr Spinder of yours as we have to tackle. That blooming blackie may make things worse by coming down on us at any moment. He's watching and waiting his time, you may depend on it, if he's this side of the water at all. Maybe he's still in India. Which'll be a mercy for us if he is. Goodbye, matey, for the present. Keep your mouth shut about having seen me.'

Sam disappeared into the darkness. Jimmy went back to the common-room again, where he found the strikers still busily engaged in discussing the proposed concert. Ram was still on the table, but no one was listening to him. The Teeth seemed to be rehearsing for the boxing exhibition which they had promised to give. Binns and Sloper were warbling unchecked. Tommy, crimson in the face, was endeavouring to obtain a hearing on the next table to Ram's. Jimmy surveyed the scene, and went out again. It was no good trying to get Tommy to himself now. If he wanted to talk things over with him he must wait till later. It may seem surprising that, after the way in which Tommy had allowed the stone to become lost, he should wish to consult him at all. But Jimmy, though he had not much opinion of Tommy's discretion, had a solid respect for his ingenuity. And it struck him that the present was an occasion where ingenuity and daring were required. There was the stone securely held by Mr Spinder. How it was to be recovered Jimmy did not know. That was where Tommy would come in. The problem was one which ought just to suit him.

It was not till they were in their room that night that he found an opportunity of tackling him on the subject. And even then he could not approach it at once, for Tommy was too full of the concert to listen.

'It's going to be the biggest thing ever done at Marleigh,' he said, as he began to undress. 'I'd no idea the place was so chockfull of talent. To look at Pilbury, for instance, you wouldn't think he was a very brainy chap, would you? Nothing out of the common, I mean. My dear chap, that fellow can imitate a pig being killed till you'd almost swear it was the real thing. Catford, too—'

'I say, Tommy.'

'Catford can do things with a top-hat which would surprise you. And, of course, Binns and Sloper are ready to go on murdering comic songs till we go on to the stage and drag them off. By the way, what are you going to do?'

'I don't know. Look here, Tommy.'

'Don't know? What rot. You must think of something. I know. You've been to India, haven't you?'

'Yes.'

'Well, you shall give a ten minutes lecture on India, accompanied by magic-lantern slides. I've got a set of slides. They're Egypt, really, but no one'll know the difference. That'll be top hole. I'll put your name down on the programme as a lightning lecturer. You'll knock 'em.'

'I say, Tommy—'

'What's up now?'

'Chuck all this concert rot for a second. I'm in an awful mess. That stone—'

'Oh, lord, you're not worrying about that still, are you? I'll get it from old Steingruber tomorrow first thing. What a chap you are for pegging away at one idea. Old Steingruber'll give it up like a shot. I'll ask him to play his 'cello. By gad!' Tommy leaped excitedly on his bed. 'I've got the idea of the century. I'll get him to play the 'cello as a turn at the concert. It'll—'

'But he hasn't got it. Do listen for a second. This is frightfully important.'

'Hasn't got it? What's he done with it? Popped it?'

'He lost it on the links.'

'Well, it wasn't much of a thing, after all. I always said so. Now it's really gone for good you can drop all this mysterious assassin rot, and turn your mind to the serious things of life, such as this concert. If only old Steingruber will play the 'cello—'

'But you haven't heard everything. He was playing with Spinder when he lost it.'

'Rum tastes some men have. Fancy choosing Spinder to play with.'

'And now Spinder's got it.'

'But you said it was lost.'

'That's the queer part of it. Spinder must have picked it up and pocketed it. I went into his room to show up some lines, and there he was, gloating over it. When he saw me, he snatched it up, shoved it in his pocket, and absolutely denied that he had got it. I knew he had, and he knew I knew, but all the same he simply swore he hadn't. So I had to go away. What I want to know is, how shall I get it back? I must somehow. I'm dashed if I see how, though.'

Tommy felt pleased. He looked at Jimmy approvingly. This was playing the game of make-believe as it should be played. So many people would have chucked the whole thing on finding that the German master had lost the stone on the links. But Jimmy, he reflected, always had been a queer, imaginative sort of fellow, always reading books, and that sort of thing. Tommy still clung to his belief that the whole affair was nothing more than an elaborate game of Jimmy's. Not so much a practical joke exactly as a means of manufacturing artificial excitement. The winter term was dull as a rule, and Jimmy was evidently determined that this one should be an exception. It was a curious sort of game, but it certainly had possibilities in the way of excitement; and that was all that Tommy required.

'I'll tell you what you must do,' he said gravely.

'What's that?'

'Search Spinder's room,' said Tommy with tremendous earnestness. 'Search it through and through. He's certain to have the stone hidden somewhere in it. This is going to be a regular Sherlock Holmes business. You've come to the right man. I'll see you through. We'll do it tonight.'

Jimmy's heart leaped. It was risky, of course, but this was no time for counting risks.

'But why should you come and risk getting caught?' he said.

Tommy dismissed the objection with a wave of the hand.

'My dear sir,' he said, 'this business is now in my hands. I'm in charge of it.'

It had evidently occurred to the person or persons who had built Marleigh School that boys might take it into their heads to break out of their rooms at night, for the arrangements for preventing this were elaborate. The boys slept in large and small dormitories at the top of the house. The only way of approach to the dormitories was by means of a long corridor at the further end of which was a blank wall. Where the corridor joined the stairs was a sort of railing, consisting of iron bars set close together. This was always locked at night by the school porter, and opened by him first thing in the morning. He slept on the same floor, to be at hand in case of fire.

To all appearances the boys, once safely behind the railings, were there for the rest of the night. Tommy Armstrong, however, had set about discovering a way through at a very early date. Unknown even to Jimmy, he had frequently broken through the barrier after lights out, and roamed about the house in the small hours.

When, therefore, Jimmy, recollecting this iron railing, objected to the proposed raiding of Mr Spinder's study on the ground that they would not be able to get at it, Tommy was full of confidence.

'Leave it to me,' he said. 'That's all I ask. Simply leave it to your uncle. He'll see you through. Now let's just think this thing over. What shall we want? In the first place, light. There's the gas, of course, but we daren't light that. It would be too risky. What we really want, what Denman Cross and all these sleuth-hound Johnnies would have had, is a dark lantern. But, as we haven't one, we must get the next best thing. By gad, I know. Bellamy's got one of those electric flashlight things you buy at Gamage's. I saw him with it the other day. It'll be in his locker down in the common-room. Our first move must be to get hold of that. Then we can start.'

'How are we going to get down to Bellamy's locker at all?'

'You'll see. By Jove, old Denman Cross would have sat on you, my lad. He'd have given you beans. Don't you know by this time that we detectives simply can't stand being questioned about our methods. All you've got to do is to stand around with your mouth open and say, "My dear Armstrong, how—" When I said that the first thing we'd got to do was to bag Bellamy's flash-jigger, I was wrong. The first thing we've got to do is to jolly well wait. It's only half-past ten, and I'll bet old Spinder is a late bird. He won't turn in till one probably. In fact, I think we'd better give him till two, to make certain.'

'What on earth are we to do till then?' asked Jimmy, rather blankly. It seemed such an age to wait. Jimmy was one of those impetuous persons who like to go at a thing without delay, and get it done at once.

'You can go to sleep,' said Tommy. 'If you chuck off all your blankets, the cold will wake you at the proper time.'

'I shan't be able to get to sleep.'

'Well, have a shot – I'm going to. Keep awake if you like; but don't jaw. Sleep is what the detective wants before taking on a job like this. It clears the brain.'

Jimmy lay awake for about a quarter of an hour, listening to Tommy's regular breathing, with a fixed conviction that sleep would never come to him. The next thing he remembered was being violently shaken. He sat up.

'Come on,' whispered Tommy, releasing his grip on his shoulder, 'it's past two. You've been snoring like blazes. I've got the whole business clearly mapped out in my mind. You've got some matches, haven't you? Good. Here's a stump of candle. Now, then.'

They went out softly into the passage. They crept along on tiptoe till they came to the railing. Then Jimmy saw that Tommy was carrying his sheet.

'What's that for?' he asked.

'You'll see. Hold the light, and stand to one side. Now, then. Life in the Wild West. Scene one: Cowboy using the lasso.'

As he spoke he whirled the sheet, which he had twisted into a sort of rope with a slip-knot at the end, up towards the ceiling. Two attempts failed, but at the third the knot caught the projecting top of one of the iron railings, and tightened.

'There you are,' said Tommy complacently. 'Scene two: Siberian convicts escaping from prison.'

He swarmed up the sheet, and, when at the top, squeezed through between the railings and the ceiling, and slid down to the floor on the other side. Jimmy, raising the light, saw that the railings stopped about two feet from the ceiling.

'Quite simple,' said Tommy through the bars. 'Only be careful when you get to the top, or you'll go scalping yourself.'

Jimmy climbed up the sheet, and joined the detective on the other side, having previously handed the candle through the railings.

'What are we to do with the sheet?' he asked.

'Pull it through the bars – like this.' Tommy suited the action to the word. 'Then leave it. Nobody's likely to be coming round here at this time of night. Now let's get going. "Once aboard the lugger, and the gyurl is mine." Don't make a row on the stairs. Look out for the fifth step. It squeaks.'

With this warning, Tommy led the way down to the common-room.

The familiar haunts seemed strange, seen at dead of night by the light of a candle. The stillness overawed Jimmy. Usually the home and centre of noise, the room was now like a tomb. The candle flung great black shadows on the wall. Even Tommy was impressed. When he spoke, it was in a whisper.

'Bit creepy, isn't it?'

Jimmy agreed. He was not nervous as a general rule, but the happenings of the last few days had shown him that life was not the quiet, uneventful thing he had always imagined it to be, but full of sinister possibilities. The knowledge that one is being watched and stalked is calculated to disturb the stoutest nerves; and Jimmy, though he had seen nothing more of the man in the train, felt convinced that he was still in the neighbourhood, waiting.

Tommy, who had nothing on his mind, was busy rummaging in Bellamy's locker, tossing about that stout youth's property in a way which would have drawn excited protests from the stolid one, had he been present. At length he rose, holding the flash-light stick.

'We are getting on,' he said, as he pressed the button and sent a thin stream of bright light shooting out. 'Now for the hidden treasure.'

He blew out the candle, and led the way to Mr Spinder's room.

'If he's still there,' he said, 'we are absolutely in the cart. I can think of an excuse for most things, but I'm blowed if I can fake up any reason why we should be wandering about the house with an electric torch at this time of night. This will mean the boot, if we are caught. So don't let's be.'

They were at the door by this time. Tommy sank noiselessly to the floor, and peered at the crack beneath the door.

'I can't see any light,' he said, rising. 'He must be in bed by now. Anyhow, here goes.'

He seized the handle, and opened the door. All was in darkness. They both breathed a sigh of relief.

'All well so far,' said Tommy. 'Let's have a bit of light on the scene once more.'

The torch came into action again. They crept silently into the room.

Mr Spinder's sitting-room was large and comfortably furnished. The light of the torch showed up deep armchairs, and their stockinged feet made no sound on the thick carpet.

'Not a bad little place by any means,' said Tommy, holding up the torch. 'Knows how to make himself comfortable, doesn't he. In old Haviland's time this room wasn't half such a blooming palace. However, we didn't come here to admire the scenery. Let's see about this stone of yours. Now, where would he keep it? Let me think. As a start we might look in each drawer of the desk.'

'They'll be locked.'

Tommy stopped.

'So they will. I never thought of that. Just shows you how easy it is for a detective to get let in. You've got to think of everything.'

'That does us,' said Jimmy. 'It's no good going on, as far as I can see. The stone's bound to be in some safe place, locked up. We'd better go back to bed.'

But Tommy was enjoying himself far too much to agree to such a tame proposition as this. He did not much care whether he found the stone or not. In fact, he did not believe that the stone was there at all. What he did care for was the opportunity of rummaging among Mr Spinder's belongings. He felt like an explorer, and did not intend to turn back now for such a thin reason as the impossibility of finding what they had set out to find.

He held the torch up, and began to prowl round the room. He stopped opposite the bookshelves.

'He's got a decent lot of books,' he said. 'Wonder if there's anything I could borrow. What's his taste in literature? What I want's a good detective story. Let's see. "Forty Years in India." "Notes on the Vedas." "Indian Mythology and Superstitions." Dash it all, the man seems to be mad on India.'

'What!' said Jimmy. 'By Jove, then that's why he's sticking to that stone. He knows all about India, and he understands what it is and why it's so valuable.'

'Not a bad theory for an amateur,' said the detective, patronisingly. 'Of course, I shall prove it absolutely wrong when once I get going on the case. Still, it's not bad.'

He walked on, and knelt before a cupboard.

'It won't be in there,' said Jimmy. 'He wouldn't keep it in a place like that.'

'I daresay he wouldn't. But he might keep biscuits. And I could do with a biscuit or two now. There, what did I tell you? A tin of the best. This is something I like. Keep trusting to the trained powers of the detective, and you can't go wrong. Do you know, something seemed to tell me there were biscuits in that cupboard. What's this? Whisky? I don't take it. But the biscuits'll do to go on with. Have one.'

'No, thanks. I wonder where he can have put that stone.'

'Never mind about the beastly stone. Sit down and— Great Scott! Listen!'

Tommy sprang to his feet, and stood listening. They looked at one another in consternation. They had both heard the sound. Soft footsteps were coming down the corridor.

There was only a moment in which to act. Whoever was coming was making his way to the study. From the stealthy way in which he was treading, it was plain that he did not wish to be heard. The same thought flashed across Jimmy and Tommy simultaneously. Mr Spinder, by some incredible bit of bad luck, had seen the sheet hanging to the railings, and was searching the house.

'There's just a chance,' whispered Tommy. 'Get behind the door. It opens inwards. Wait till he's in, then make a bolt for it before he lights the gas.'

As luck would have it, there was a settee against the wall at the side of the door. There was no time to drag it out, even if such an action would not have made too much noise.

'The piano,' whispered Jimmy.

Tommy nodded. The piano – the favourite possession of Mr Haviland, who had been an enthusiastic musician – stood in the corner of the room beyond the settee. It was so placed that each side of it touched one wall, thus leaving a small triangular space between the instrument and the corner. There would be just room for them to squeeze behind it. And, once there, they might be safe. It was a poor chance, if the man who was coming down the passage was Mr Spinder searching the house. But still, it was a chance, and the only one they could take.

They dashed towards it. The next moment they were behind it, and Tommy had switched off the light.

Hardly had he done so when the footsteps paused at the door. Then, though there was no sound, they knew that the man, whoever he was, had entered the room.

There was a slight click, and a circle of light appeared on the ceiling, darting off again at once. At the same time the smell of hot tin came to them. Tommy gave Jimmy a nudge. They knew what had happened. The man had uncovered a dark lantern.

This disposed of the idea that the man was Mr Spinder. A master who is searching his house with the object of finding boys who may be wandering in it during the night does not do it with the aid of a dark lantern. Nor does he walk on tiptoe. The fact that the visitor was doing both these things put an entirely new complexion on the affair. It showed that he had as little business to be in Mr Spinder's study at that hour as had the two boys crouching behind the piano.

Tommy, squeezing Jimmy's shoulder as a sign to him to keep still, rose cautiously to his feet till he could see above the top of the piano. The light had disappeared from their limited range of vision.

Very warily Tommy looked out from his hiding-place. Then he saw that there was no need for excessive caution. The man had his back towards him. He was kneeling in front of Mr Spinder's desk. The lantern was on the floor beside him.

The position of the lantern made it hard for Tommy to see exactly what was happening. The man seemed to be doing something to the desk, and he seemed to be doing it under difficulties. Then another click told him what was going on. The man was breaking open the drawers with a skeleton key.

As Tommy watched, he pulled the top drawer from its place, and, laying it on the floor beside the lantern, began to rummage among its contents. He used one hand only for this, and, as the light fell on him, Tommy saw the reason. His left arm was in a sling.

Tommy gazed, spellbound. Here was an adventure of the type

he had always longed for. Standing there, peering over the piano, was like watching a very exciting play on the stage.

Whatever the man was looking for, it was evidently not in the top drawer. After an exhaustive examination of its contents, he put it carefully back in its place, and re-locked it. Then he took out the second drawer, and began his search once more. All the while he made no sound that could be heard outside the room. An occasional deep breath escaped him, and the papers in the drawer rustled faintly; but beyond that the silence was unbroken. His patience seemed inexhaustible. He was plainly bent on finding the object of his search, for, when the second drawer yielded nothing, he replaced it and turned to the next in order without a sign of discouragement.

For nearly half an hour Tommy reckoned that he stood there watching, with a hand always on Jimmy's shoulder to check any attempt the latter might think of making to rise and join him in his vigil. There was no room behind the piano for two people to move about.

Still with the same patience, the man went through each of the drawers in turn, till he came to the last. That, too, was searched from end to end. He replaced it, locked it, and rose to his feet. As he did so Tommy dropped silently back on to the floor.

The light moved about the room. It was still moving, when the two boys, listening intently, heard another sound, faint but distinct. This time it came from the direction of the window.

The man with the lantern had evidently heard it, too. There was a click, and the light disappeared.

Tommy and Jimmy hardly breathed as they listened. The sound continued. It was a very faint scratching noise, as if somebody were cutting at the window-pane. Then the sound ceased, to be followed almost at once by the rasp of the catch as it was forced back.

They understood now what had happened. Somebody had cut out a pane of glass with a diamond, and, having thrust a hand through the opening, had pushed back the catch. That this surmise was correct was proved by the noise of the window being pushed very slowly up. A cold breath of air came into the room. They could hear sounds which suggested that someone was climbing cautiously in over the sill.

Then suddenly there was a slither of feet on the carpet, the thud of a blow, a cry of mingled pain and surprise, and then the bumping of two heavy bodies on the floor.

'I've got you now,' gasped a voice. 'I'll pay you for those bullets of yours.'

'It's Sam!' cried Jimmy, unable to check himself in his excitement.

Tommy pinched his arm hard; but neither of the two men fighting out in the room beyond the piano appeared to have heard the words. They were struggling silently now, as far as speaking was concerned; but as they rolled on the floor they crashed now into a chair, now into a table, till the air seemed full of the noise of their struggles.

'Great Scott,' whispered Tommy, as a small bookstand fell with a crash into the fender, waking the echoes, 'somebody's bound to hear this row pretty soon.'

Jimmy half rose.

'We must go and help,' he said excitedly. 'Let me go. It's Sam. He won't stand a chance with that shoulder of his.'

But Tommy continued to hold him down.

'Don't be an idiot,' he whispered. 'Don't you stir, or we're done for. Spinder or someone will be down in a second. They're making row enough to wake the dead. Listen to that! That must have been the chair with the biscuit tin on it! They'll have the roof off in a minute.'

'But Sam will be killed.'

'No, he won't. Not much sign of it yet, at any rate,' he added, as a deep curse from the other man showed that Sam's strength had by no means failed as yet. 'We mustn't risk being caught here. There would be a frightful row. We should get the boot tomorrow. We must simply sit tight here till it's all over. Hullo! Do you hear that?'

From down the corridor came the sound of voices.

'This way, Bartlett, this way.'

The voice was Mr Spinder's. Bartlett was the school porter, a muscular ex-soldier, who, as stated above, slept in a room at the top of the house close to the iron railings.

'Right, sir,' came Bartlett's gruff voice.

'This way,' cried Mr Spinder again. 'In my study.'

The sound of running footsteps came nearer and nearer.

'Sit tight,' whispered Tommy, clutching Jimmy by the arm. 'Don't breathe. We're in a tight place.'

The fight on the floor ceased abruptly. As if by mutual consent the two men loosed their hold of each other, and sprang to their feet. The next moment Sam's antagonist, leaping through the window, had vanished into the night; and Sam followed his example just as the others dashed into the room. Mr Spinder, entering first, was just in time to see Sam's back as he dropped over the sill. Bartlett, the porter, was for following him, but Mr Spinder held him back.

'It is useless, Bartlett,' he said. 'They have gone.'

'I might 'ave caught one of 'em, sir,' said Bartlett.

'No, no. There is no need to run risks of that kind. Close the window, Bartlett, will you? Thank you. Have you a match? Thank you. I will just light the gas, and have a look round to see if the scoundrels have taken anything.'

There was the splutter of a match, and the light of the gas flooded the room, making the two boys behind the piano blink as the glare struck their eyes.

'Lord, sir,' came Bartlett's voice. 'They 'aven't 'arf played old Harry with the furniture!'

Tommy and Jimmy could hear him moving about the room, picking up the various tables and chairs which Sam and the other man had upset in their struggles. When he had completed this task, Mr Spinder spoke: 'That will do excellently, Bartlett. Thank you. I don't think those fellows have taken anything.

I don't think there is any need to keep you any longer from your bed. Perhaps you would like a little—'

'Thank you, sir,' said Bartlett's voice, in what seemed to the two boys rather relieved accents.

There followed the splashing of liquid into a glass, and a murmured 'Best of 'ealth, sir,' from Bartlett.

'Good-night, Bartlett,' said Mr Spinder.

'Good-night, sir.'

'Oh – and, Bartlett.'

'Yes, sir.'

'I think there will be no need of gossip, you understand, about this affair. I would prefer that you said nothing to anybody on the subject.'

'Said nothing to nobody, sir!' Bartlett seemed taken aback at the idea. He had plainly been counting on the episode to furnish him with interesting conversation for weeks to come in the servants' hall.

'Not a word. There is no need to do so, and it would only make a great deal of fuss and trouble. Nothing has been taken. No harm has been done. So let us allow the matter to drop.'

'Yes, sir,' said Bartlett gloomily.

'Very well. Then good-night, Bartlett.'

'Good-night, sir.'

They heard the porter's steps retreating down the passage.

When he had gone, Mr Spinder stayed so still for a while that, if Tommy and Jimmy had not known that he was there, they might well have thought that the room was empty.

At the end, however, of what seemed an age, they heard him move towards the door. He closed it, and walked slowly back to the centre of the room. Here he paused again; finally moving to the big bookshelf that stood against the wall.

He was completely hidden from Jimmy; but Tommy, who was crouching against the same wall as that at which the bookshelf was placed, could follow his movements, which were curious. After standing for some time apparently buried in thought, the master took from the shelf a large book in the second row.

Tommy, who was following his every movement intently, saw that it was either the fifth or sixth book from the end of the shelf. That he had not taken it out with any idea of reading it was soon apparent, for he laid it on a chair at his side, and thrust his hand into the gap between the books. He felt about for a moment, and then withdrew his hand. He looked at some small object in it with satisfaction, and replaced it. Then, having put back the book, he turned out the gas, and left the room.

'Phew!' said Tommy, as the door closed. 'I like excitement, but one can have too much of a good thing. This business has been altogether too hot for your uncle. After all, one's handicapped at school when one tries to work the detective act. Sherlock Holmes wasn't wondering the whole time that he was hunting for clues whether he would get expelled. That's what does one in. It hampers one.'

'Is it safe to get up?' asked Jimmy. 'Anyhow, I'm going to. I've got cramp.'

'Get up as much as you like. Only don't make too much row about it. Spinder's just the snaky sort of brute who might be hanging about outside the door. By Jove, what a turn-up those two chaps had! I wish we could have seen it.'

'I wonder that brute didn't kill Sam, considering that Sam had only one arm to fight with.'

'Are you certain it was Sam?'

'Positive. I knew his voice in a second.'

'Rum thing. One second.'

Tommy wriggled out of his hiding-place, turned on the electric torch, and went to the bookshelf. He took out the sixth book from the end of the second row, and thrust his hand into the opening, as Mr Spinder had done. But, beyond getting his fingers very dusty, he accomplished nothing.

'Rum thing,' he said. 'I could have sworn I saw him put it back.'

'What's up?' asked Jimmy.

'Nothing. Look here, we'd better be getting back to bed. I don't suppose that sheet of ours will be spotted, but it might be, and then the whole game would be up. Come on.'

They opened the door cautiously, and crept down the passage.

'Better put this torch-thing back,' said Tommy. 'If Bellamy missed it tomorrow there might be a row.'

They went to the common-room, and restored the electric torch to its locker. Then they crept upstairs.

The sheet was still in its place. Tommy pulled it through the bars, and climbed over the railing. Jimmy followed his example, unhooking the improvised rope when he had reached the top.

'Well,' said Tommy thankfully, as they got into bed, 'we're well out of that. If that's a sample of a night in this house now that Spinder's in command, I shall jolly well chuck going about after lights-out. It isn't good enough. Now I'm going to try and get a bit of sleep. Goodness knows what the time is. It's not worthwhile striking a light and looking. It must be about three. I'm aching all over from squatting behind that beastly piano. Goodnight.'

'Good-night,' said Jimmy. But he did not go to sleep. Tommy's breathing soon became heavy and regular. Tommy was the sort of person who could get to sleep in five minutes whenever he wanted to; but Jimmy's mind was in a whirl. The events of the night had left him utterly perplexed. Who was the man with whom Sam had grappled? Was it the man who had travelled down with Tommy and himself in the train? If so, what had brought him to Mr Spinder's room? How did he know that the stone was in the master's possession?

Sam's movements were more easily to be accounted for. Jimmy had shown him which was Mr Spinder's room; and it was not to be wondered at that Sam had conceived the idea of making an attempt to recover the blue stone for himself.

But what of his antagonist? That problem kept Jimmy perplexed. The fact that Sam had attacked him, added to his words as he grappled with him, showed that Sam had taken him for one of the gang who had been tracking him. But why was he in Mr Spinder's room?

A possible solution of the mystery occurred to him after much thought. Mr Spinder's was the only window on the ground floor of the building which was not heavily barred. It was, in fact, the only way in for a burglar. Probably the man had intended to use it simply as a means of entrance, before proceeding to search the house. His, Jimmy's, room must have been his ultimate goal.

Mr Spinder's part in the affair had now become doubly sinister. It was now evident that he not only realised the value of the blue stone, but was prepared to keep it in his possession at any cost. His manner had almost suggested that he had expected some such attempt. His instructions, also, to Bartlett to say nothing of the matter showed this plainly. It was clear that it was now war to the knife, a triangular contest with the blue stone as the prize. The atmosphere was charged with veiled hints of danger.

Having arrived at these conclusions, Jimmy fell asleep, and did not wake till Bartlett, as was his custom, opened the iron railing and walked up and down the corridor ringing the getting-up bell.

The majority of people, having gone through what Tommy Armstrong had endured in the way of adventure overnight, would probably have chosen to lie low on the following day, thinking that they had had enough excitement for the time being. Tommy's appetite, however, was accustomed to grow by what it fed on. A little episode like crouching for an hour or so behind a piano, while two burglars entered the housemaster's study, fought on the floor, and were eventually surprised and routed by the housemaster in person, simply gave Tommy the pleasing feeling that he was living his life as it should be lived. So far from being tired of excitement, he looked about him for the means of manufacturing a further supply.

The instrument was ready to his hand, in the shape of Simpson's rabbit, Blib. The success of his previous experiment in letting this animal loose in the class-room encouraged him to try the experiment again. Not with Mr Spinder, who had been present during Blib's previous visit to the class-room – for Tommy never liked to overdo a thing – but with Herr Steingruber. Piquancy would be added to the situation by the fact that the Herr hated rabbits.

The scheme was, however, wrecked by the unsympathetic attitude of Simpson. Tommy approached him after breakfast.

'I say, Simpson,' he said. 'You know, those rabbits of yours don't get nearly enough exercise.'

'You've raced them in the passage pretty well every night since the beginning of term. I don't know what more you want.'

'Yes, that's all right as far as it goes, but it doesn't go nearly far enough. A few sprints up and down a passage aren't half enough for a healthy rabbit. What they want is a run in the daytime.'

'If you mean—' began Simpson suspiciously.

'I was thinking,' said Tommy airily, 'that if you could lend me Blib for the German lesson—'

'I'm blowed if I do. You got the poor brute confiscated last time, and it was only by a fluke that I got him back at all. I'm not going to risk it again.'

'Oh, I say, Simpson, don't be a cad.'

'I'm hanged if you shall have my rabbit. If you want to bring anything into the class-room, why don't you borrow Blackie?'

Tommy paused. It was not a bad suggestion. Blackie, the house cat, was a stately animal, whose mission in life was supposed to be the catching of mice. He spent most of his time, however, asleep in the kitchen. Whether he worked while others slept, and made a great slaughter of mice in the small hours of the night, nobody knew. But he could be counted on to have no engagements during the day.

'I will,' said Tommy.

By good luck he chanced to meet Blackie patrolling the passage near the dining-room directly after breakfast. He proceeded to commandeer him.

When Herr Steingruber entered the class-room, Blackie, soothed by a saucer of milk, was asleep in Tommy's desk.

The German master was in his most jovial mood.

'Ach, my liddle vriendts,' he said, 'zo we are again for der ztudying of der Sherman language med dogedder. Led us now broceed our acguaindance with der verbs und deir gurious irregularities do resume. Jutwell, my vriendt, vill you der—'

He stopped abruptly, and 'pointed' like a dog.

'Ach,' he said, 'dell me, is dere in der room a gat?'

It so happened that Herr Steingruber, like Lord Roberts and other famous men, had a constitutional loathing for cats. This curious weakness which attacks some people has never been properly explained, but it undoubtedly exists. Something tells these men when there is a cat in the room, even though they cannot see it.

'A gat, sir?' asked Chutwell.

'Jah. A mitz. A – you know – a gat. I am zure by der gurious veeling in my inzides dot dere was a gat in der room.'

The German master's moustache was bristling. His eyes gleamed in an agitated way behind his spectacles. Suddenly a well-known sound came from the interior of Tommy's desk. The Herr started like a war-horse that has heard the trumpet.

'Dere! Did you nod id hear?'

'Hear, sir? What, sir?'

'Der gat-like mewing zound.'

'It might have been a desk squeaking, sir,' suggested Tommy. 'Sometimes the nuts get loose, and—'

'No, no, it vos not der desg, it vos der gat-like mewing, dot id vos do mistake imbossible. Ach! Again! Did you nod thad dime id hear?'

This time it was out of the question to deny it. Blackie, having finished his sleep, and finding to his consternation that he was in a sort of wooden box, far too small to give him room to move with any comfort, was now expressing his disgust and disapproval in no uncertain voice. Though muffled by the lid of the desk, the yowls were more than plainly audible.

The class decided on a compromise.

'It *does* sound like a cat, sir,' agreed Browning. 'It's probably outside in the road.'

'I'm not sure it's not a sort of bird, sir,' said Tommy, unwilling to concede even as much as Browning. 'There are birds which make a noise just like that.'

'No, no, you are nod right, neither of you, my liddle vellows,' said the German master excitedly. 'Id vos der gat, nod der bird; und id vos in der room, nod in der road oudside. Ach!' He turned towards Tommy. 'Armstrong, der gat-like mewing from der direction of you zeems do gome.'

'Me, sir!' said Tommy.

The Herr dashed towards him like a hound that has struck the trail, and stopped in a listening attitude. Tommy leaned heavily on his desk.

'Armstrong,' said the Herr, 'berhaps der gat behind der gupboard door is goncealed. Go und loog, my Armsdrong.'

There was a small cupboard against the wall, in which exercise-books, chalk, and other things were kept.

'I don't think it can be in there, sir.'

'But berhabs id is. Examine der gupboard, my boy.'

Tommy rose from his seat, and by so doing gave Blackie his chance. The lid, released from the pressure of his arm, rose slowly. The cries increased in volume. For a moment Herr Steingruber did not notice what was happening to the desk. Then it caught his eye, and, as he would have put it himself, he crouched and sprang. He seized the lid of the desk, and flung it open.

'Ach!' he cried. 'Zo! As I zusbegded!'

Then he uttered a howl compared with which those of the

imprisoned cat were as nothing; for Blackie, rising slowly from his place, gave a sudden spring on to Herr Steingruber's head, and stood there spitting.

The Herr sprang back, and began to rush about the room like a madman.

'Dake id off! Dake id my head off!'

The class rose from its place as one man. A dozen willing hands removed the indignant Blackie from his perch, and hustled him out of the door. The German master sank into his seat, gasping.

'How it managed to get in there, sir—' began Tommy.

His voice roused the Herr from his stupor.

'Ach, vile Armsdrong,' he roared. 'Sgoundrel! Villain! You will for me von tausand lines write. Ach! Dot vill you deach anudder dime not to in der desg with gunning and wickedness der gat blace. Sgoundrel boy!'

Tommy knew better than to protest at the time. He had seen the Herr like this before, and he knew how to deal with the situation. He resumed his seat quietly, and for the rest of the lesson could have given a lamb points in meekness and docility.

When the lesson was over, and the room empty, he crept to the German master's desk.

'Please, sir.'

'Vell, Armsdrong.'

The Herr's voice was stiff with righteous indignation.

'I came to say how sorry I was for—'

'Ach! Doo lade id is for der zorrow und rebendance. You should of dot have before thought. Von tausand lines you will write.'

'Oh, yes, sir,' said Tommy eagerly. 'I didn't want you to let me off the lines. All I wanted was to tell you how sorry I was.'

'Dot vos der right sbirit, Armsdrong,' said the Herr, slightly softened.

'I don't know how I came to do it, sir. I found the cat in the passage, and brought him in without thinking.'

'Always should you dthink, my boy,' said Herr Steingruber ponderously. 'As your boet says, Moch evil has been wrought by want of dhought. Jah, zo.'

'Yes, sir.'

'There was just one other thing, sir,' added Tommy.

Just then the door opened. Mr Spinder appeared.

'Ah, the class is over? I thought I should find Stewart here. Armstrong, kindly tell Stewart that a visitor is waiting for him in the drawing-room.'

'Yes, sir.'

Mr Spinder disappeared. Tommy returned to his subject.

'There was just one thing, sir.'

'Vhot vos dot?'

'It's like this, sir. We are getting up a concert for – for a charitable object. We are all of us going to do something. Some of us will sing, and some recite, and some conjure, and so on.'

'Jah, zo,' said Herr Steingruber, nodding. 'I zee. Der zocial goncert for der goot object. Zo.'

'We've got a very strong programme, but we all agreed that it would be simply topping—'

'Dopping?'

'You know, sir – great, splendid.'

'Jah, zo.'

'If you would only come and play us something on your 'cello.'

The Herr's face lit up. He loved his 'cello, which, it may be mentioned, he played really well. His demeanour relaxed at once. All the righteous indignation vanished. He patted Tommy on the head.

'Ach! Zo you vish me on der violoncello do blay, is id? Ach, but shall I nod – you know – what you would zay zboil der fun? You will be der merry lads zinging und choking. Should I nod be in der way, my liddle man?'

For the first time in his life Tommy became aware that he possessed a conscience. He had intended originally to get the Herr to play at the concert with a view to a tremendous rag. The German master's words made him alter his mind swiftly and completely.

'Of course you won't, sir,' he said with sincerity. 'We shall all be awfully glad if you would play. And,' he added to himself, 'if any of those fools try to rag you, I'll knock their heads off.'

'I shall with bleasure blay,' said Herr Steingruber.

'Thank you, sir. That's all I wanted to ask you.'

'Ach, but sdob, Armsdrong, sdob. Berhabs a liddle doo severe I was on der boyish biece of fon. Der tausand lines I do gancel. But anodder dime, my boy, do nod der gat indo der glass-room bring.'

'No, sir. Thank you very much, sir.'

Tommy departed to find Jimmy, whom he discovered in the common-room, and despatched in quest of his visitor.

Jimmy wondered, as he went to the drawing-room, who this visitor could be. There was nobody he knew who was likely to come and see him at school. He arrived at the drawing-room, and opened the door. A man was standing, looking out of the window. As Jimmy came in, he turned round, and advanced with a smile.

Jimmy stood still, staring. It was the man who had travelled down with Tommy and himself in the train.

That the visitor did not imagine that there would be any danger of Jimmy recognising him was evident from his manner. And there was certainly some excuse for this confidence, for he was as cunningly 'made up' as an actor on the stage. When Jimmy had seen him in the train, his hair had been jet-black, and he had been clean-shaven. The man who stood before Jimmy now was grey-haired, and his mouth was covered by a heavy grey moustache. He carried himself like a soldier, and looked exactly like any one of a score of retired officers you might meet at a service club.

But Jimmy had a wonderful memory for faces, inherited from his father. However the man in the train might have altered his appearance, one feature remained the same – the eyes. Jimmy had never forgotten the keen, sinister eyes which had looked at him through the window on the night Sam had been shot down. They had burned themselves into his memory. And this man had those eyes.

'Well, my boy,' said the man in a bluff, good-humoured way, holding out his hand, 'so you're young Jimmy, are you? Bless my soul, how you've grown. Why, when last I saw you, you were in your ayah's arms, squealing like a steam engine. You don't remember me, of course.'

'No,' said Jimmy. Which was strictly untrue.

'Of course not, of course not. How should you? We had very little conversation on that occasion, if I remember rightly. I showed you my watch, and you kicked me in the stomach, and then you were taken upstairs. And we never met again. But I saw a good deal of your father. We were in the same regiment, you know. Brother officers, and always the greatest of chums. You have probably heard him speak of me? Marshall. Major Marshall. Dear old Stewart! We used to call him Babe. I'm sure I don't know why, for he was anything but one. Have you seen your father lately? Saw him in the holidays, I suppose, eh?'

Jimmy had an uncomfortable feeling that this man was beginning to pump him for information, and he wondered uneasily how far he would go. He was bristling with suspicion. However, there seemed no harm in answering his questions so far.

'No,' he said. 'Father is away.'

'Away? Dear me, that's a nuisance. I was hoping to see him, and have a chat about the old days. Where is he?'

'In Africa.'

'Africa! Well, I can hardly go over there, can I? I'd no idea. Are you expecting him back soon?'

Jimmy swiftly examined this question with a view to seeing how his answer would affect Major Marshall in his designs on the blue stone. If he said his father was returning to England soon, it would cause Marshall to redouble his efforts to obtain the stone before Colonel Stewart's arrival. If, on the other hand, Marshall thought that he had plenty of time, he might go about his work in a more leisurely manner.

It seemed to Jimmy that, with the stone still in Mr Spinder's possession, the great thing was to gain time. The fact that Sam Burrows had broken into the house and searched the master's room showed that the former was prepared to go to any length to recover the lost stone, and, if given time, would probably hit on some scheme for regaining possession of it. So Jimmy replied that he had not heard from his father for some time, and that he did not expect him back for another month – possibly more.

The answer seemed to satisfy Marshall. His voice, when he spoke, was more good-humoured than ever.

'He always was fond of sport,' he said. 'When we were in India together, he was always getting leave, and plunging off into the jungle after tigers. First-rate shot he was. I expect he's enjoying himself far too much in Africa to dream of coming back. Well, well, all we can do, my boy, is to console ourselves in the mean-time with each other's company. Suppose you put on your hat, and come to the tuck-shop with me, eh?'

Jimmy, keenly on his guard, scented danger.

This man knew nothing of Mr Spinder, and imagined that he, Jimmy, still held the stone in his keeping. Jimmy was not going to give him the opportunity of getting him alone. Here, on the school premises, he was safe. Nothing could touch him. But, if once he left his ground, anything might have happened. He excused himself, politely but resolutely.

'Thanks awfully,' he said, 'but I'm afraid I shouldn't be allowed to go out now. It isn't a half-holiday. I shall have to be going into school again soon.'

'Oh, nonsense, my boy, nonsense. I'll soon get permission for you. I'll see your master. What's his name? Spinder? I'll see Mr Spinder, and ask if you can't come out for half an hour.'

'It's no good. He wouldn't let me.'

'Ah, well, discipline, discipline! A fine thing! We must all obey orders, mustn't we. It would never do if we were allowed to come and go just as we pleased, would it?'

Jimmy said nothing. Major Marshall picked up his hat and stick.

'Ah, by the way,' said the Major, 'I knew there was something else. Of course, yes. Who should I come across the other day but Corporal Burrows, of your father's and my old regiment. Hadn't seen him for an age. A fine soldier, Burrows. I have had him at my side in some tight corners.'

This, thought Jimmy, thinking of the happenings of the previous night, was quite true.

'He was very glad to see me, was Burrows. It seems that he left India with a commission to hand over a certain stone either to your father or myself; and it upset the poor fellow when he found that your father was not in England.'

'Did Burrows tell you my father was not in England?'

'Yes. Poor fellow, I think he had been worrying himself about it.'

'Then why did you ask me where he was?' said Jimmy.

Major Marshall's face changed; but he recovered himself quickly, and laughed.

'You're a sharp youngster,' he said, smiling. 'Uncommonly sharp. The fact is, I'd forgotten all about Burrows for the moment. He only came into my mind as I was leaving.'

'Then it isn't very important about the stone?'

'Oh, no. Burrows upset himself quite unnecessarily.'

'I'm glad of that,' said Jimmy.

'It's of very little importance, really. But those men like Burrows, when they are entrusted with any commission, magnify it till in their eyes it becomes quite an international business.'

'I see,' said Jimmy.

'Burrows tells me he handed the stone over to you, to keep till you saw your father. Fortunately, now that I've met him, it isn't necessary to wait any longer. You can give it to me, and then poor Burrows' mind will be set at rest.'

'Do you think that's really what Sam Burrows would want me to do?'

'Of course, my boy, of course. What else? It would be the greatest relief to him.'

'Then what were you and he fighting about in the study last night?'

The words had left Jimmy's lips before he had time to think. When the thing was done, he would have given much to be able to recall them. He blamed himself bitterly for being such a fool as to yield to the temptation to score off Marshall; but the other's bluff, plausible manner had been too much for him. He could see now what a mistake he had made. Marshall, on his guard and knowing that Jimmy was on his guard, was a far more formidable foe than a Marshall who imagined that his motives were unsuspected.

There was a long silence. The pupils of Marshall's eyes contracted like those of a snake. Jimmy backed slowly against the wall. Marshall was between him and the door, or he would have run for it.

At length Marshall spoke. His voice had lost all its bluff cheeriness. Instead, it had taken on a deadly coldness. Jimmy, plucky as he was, trembled when he heard it.

'Enough of this nonsense,' said Marshall. 'I see you know more than I thought. Give me that stone.'

Jimmy said nothing. He was against the wall now. He licked his lips, which were feeling curiously dry.

'Be quick,' said Marshall. 'If you know as much as you seem to, you'll know that I mean business. Where's that stone?'

Jimmy, rigid against the wall, was aware of something hard

pressing into the small of his back. His heart gave a bound as it flashed across him what this thing was. It was the electric-bell button, which stood out from the wall in its wooden case.

He slid a hand silently up the wall till he found it. Then he pressed with all the force he could muster.

Marshall had not seen the movement; or, if he had, had not understood its meaning.

'I'll give you ten seconds to produce that stone. If I've not got it by then—' He snarled out an oath.

Still Jimmy made no reply. His ear had caught the sound of footsteps in the passage. Marshall had heard them, too. He stopped as he was advancing, and looked over his shoulder.

The door opened, and a servant appeared. She seemed astonished, as well she might, for Jimmy's ringing had been urgent enough to wake the Seven Sleepers.

'Did you ring, sir?' she asked.

Marshall resumed his bluff manner like a garment.

'My young friend here did,' he said genially. 'No need to have rung the house down, Jimmy, my boy. I merely wished you to tell Mr Spinder that I have had to hurry off to catch a train. Will you do this? Thank you. Well, Jimmy, my boy, I must say goodbye. Very glad to have been able to see you.'

Their eyes met as they shook hands. Jimmy could see that Marshall's were still cold and furious. There was something particularly horrible in the combination of those vicious eyes and the genial, soldierly manner.

'I hope we shall meet again very soon,' said Marshall. 'In fact,' he added, turning as he reached the door, 'I am sure we shall. Quite sure.'

Jimmy waited till he had left the room. Then he tottered to a chair and sat down. He was feeling sick.

'I say,' said Tommy Armstrong, coming into the common-room on the following morning. 'Heard the latest? Those college chaps want us to play them at football!'

'Play the college!'

'Their second eleven. I've just heard from a cousin of mine who's there. He's captain of their second eleven this year, and a most awful ass. Sticks on side enough for a dozen, too. I can't stand the man.'

'What does he say?'

'I'll read it. "I wonder if your fellows could manage to scratch up an eleven—" '

'Scratch up an eleven!' cried the common-room indignantly.

'That's what he says.'

'Dash it all, does he think we've never heard of footer?'

'Does he think we play marbles here, or what?'

'Doesn't he know we beat Burlingford Wednesday Reserves last year by a goal to nil?'

'Your cousin wants kicking, Tommy.'

'So I always tell him when I see him,' said Tommy with composure. 'This is how he goes on. Let me see, where was I? Ah, "Scratch up an eleven to play our second on the sixteenth. We were to have played the Emeriti on that day, but they have disappointed us. Can you get together eleven fellows from your place who know a football from a croquet ball—?"'

Here the audience interposed again.

'I never heard such cheek in my life.'

'Beastly side!'

'These college fools seem to think that just because—'

'By the side of the Zuyder Zee, Zuy—'

'Oh, sit on that ass Binns, for goodness' sake.'

'Don't trouble,' said the songster. 'I desist. I was merely rehearsing for the concert. Sloper, my lad.'

'What ho?'

'What sort of voice are you in?'

'Poor, I fear. A trifle ropy. And you?'

'A little weak in the upper register. But we shall be all right on the night.'

'Rather. Buck along, Tommy. We're all listening.'

'Oh, you've finished, have you?' said Tommy. 'Struck one of your brilliant flashes of silence? That's good. I'll go on, then. "Football from a croquet ball? If so, bring them along. We shan't expect anything great. The idea is simply to give our chaps a bit of practice, and prevent them getting out of form."'

'Oh, is it?'

'Jolly good of them to play with beginners like us, I *don't* think.'

'We shall pick up the rules as we go along.'

'"Getting out of form,"' resumed Tommy. '"You can play masters if you like."'

'Can we? By Jove! that's kind of them.'

'Awfully kind.'

'We'll bring old Steingruber.'

'He'd be pretty hot in goal. Couldn't get much past him. There'd be no room.'

'Or Spinder.'

Roars of laughter greeted this suggestion.

'"Yours sincerely, J. de V. Patterne,"' concluded Tommy. '"P.S. You might send one of your fellows over today to let us know. If I don't hear from you today, I shall conclude that you can't raise a team, and shall make other arrangements."'

'So that's your cousin, is it, Tommy?'

'It is,' replied Tommy sadly. 'But we hush it up in our family as much as possible. It's a very sad business. Well, there you are. What do you think about it? Are you on? Shall we play them?'

'Rather!'

'What do *you* think?'

'If we don't, they'll think we funk them.'

'We'll give them beans.'

'Right ho,' said Tommy. 'I'll put up the list of our team tonight.' Tommy captained the Marleigh School football eleven. He and Jimmy played back together, and formed a pair whose defence took a lot of breaking. 'We shall have to go into strict training for it. We simply must win. Jimmy, will you bike over this afternoon, and see my cousin about it, and arrange things?'

'All right,' said Jimmy.

'Anybody else care to go?' asked Tommy.

Everybody wanted to go, and said so simultaneously.

'Take old Ram,' said Tommy. 'He'll astonish their weak intellects.'

Ram beamed with pleasure at the compliment.

'I shall be proud and puffed-up as a peacock,' he said, 'to be your spokesman and *amicus curiæ*.'

Alderton College was a large public school which lay about five miles from Marleigh School. The boys of the two schools did not come into contact with one another very frequently, but when they did there was generally trouble. The Marleigh boys looked on the Alderton brigade, not without some reason, as giving themselves airs. Sometimes, when a Marleigh paper-chase met an Alderton cross-country run on neutral territory, there would be something in the nature of a free fight. It was on one of these occasions that Jimmy had engaged in a contest of words with a red-headed Aldertonian, and had scored off him with such completeness that the latter was proceeding to turn the thing from a verbal to a physical battle, when one of the college masters arrived, and separated them.

This, indeed, was the chief reason why Jimmy had consented to go to the college to arrange about the match. He did not wish it to be thought – not that it was likely to be thought, for nobody at Marleigh had ever questioned Jimmy's courage – that he was avoiding Alderton for fear of meeting the red-headed one. But for this he might have backed out of going, for, plucky as he was, the scene with Major Marshall in the drawing-room had shaken him, and he would have preferred to have stayed within the safe bounds of the school. There was a strong likelihood that he would be watched; and if it came to a pinch, Ram would not be much of a help.

But, taking everything into consideration, he determined to risk it; and, directly after school was over, he and Ram, mounted on bicycles, made their way to the college.

A small boy in the cap of one of the houses at the college was lounging in the road outside the big gates when they arrived.

'I say,' said Jimmy, 'can you tell me where to find Patterne?'

The small boy did not answer the question; but, having eyed Jimmy's school cap in a lofty manner, proceeded to gaze spell-bound at Ram, who stood beaming at him through his gold spectacles.

At this moment a second small boy in a similar cap came through the gates. The first small boy drew his attention to Ram, and the two of them fixed him with an unblinking stare.

'Misters,' said Ram, 'I—'

The two small boys started violently.

'Golly! You made me jump!' said one.

'You might have told us it could talk,' said the other complainingly, to Jimmy.

'We don't want any of your cheek,' said Jimmy crisply.

The two small boys transferred their attention to him.

'Who are you?' said one.

'When you're at home,' added the other.

'Where can I find Patterne?' asked Jimmy again.

'Young sirs,' broke in Ram, 'are you the ninnies or the beetle-headed chaps that you remain *sotto-voce* and hermetically sealed? Why do you fob us off with the disrespectful superciliousness of the cold shoulder? Hoity-toity, young chaps, is this your boasted British courtesy? Tell us where can we find Hon'ble Patterne?'

'How does it work?' asked the first small boy, turning to Jimmy. 'Do you shove a penny in the slot?'

'Oh, come on, Ram,' said Jimmy. 'We're wasting time. They oughtn't to allow these kids out without their nurses.'

They wheeled their bicycles in through the big gates and across the quadrangle. Groups of boys were strolling about, some in football clothes, on their way to the field, others in the blue coats and grey flannel trousers, which was the customary wear at the college. At first Jimmy and his companion attracted no attention. Then somebody caught sight of Ram, and presently they were in the centre of a large group.

'Why are you two chaps strolling about in here as if you'd bought the place?'

'Where's the rest of the circus?'

'It's the Shah! Somebody ought to tell the Old Man; we may get a half on the strength of it. Royal visit to Alderton.'

'We've come from Marleigh,' began Jimmy.

'You look it.'

Jimmy was beginning to lose his temper, but he showed no sign of it. He went on patiently.

'Patterne wrote to our skipper, asking if we would play your second eleven. We've come over to arrange about the match. Can you tell me where I can find Patterne?'

'Here he is,' said one of the group. 'Hi, Pat!'

'What's up?'

A long, languid youth, dressed with rather more care than the average run of Aldertonians, strolled up, arm-in-arm with a sturdy, thickset boy in a blue and brown cap. Jimmy recognised him at once. It was his friend of the red hair.

The latter did not recognise him in turn for some little time. It was not till Patterne had been discussing with Jimmy details of the forthcoming match in a tired drawl for some moments that he made the great discovery. When he did he stepped forward.

'Well, look heah,' Patterne was saying, when the other interrupted him.

'One second, Pat. I say,' to Jimmy, 'you've seen me before.'

'We all have our troubles,' said Jimmy.

'You're the lout who cheeked me.'

'And you're the silly ass who couldn't think of anything to say back.'

The red-haired one drew a step nearer. He and Jimmy were quite close to each other now.

The rest of the group looked on, interested. The situation seemed to promise sport.

'I owe you a licking,' said the red-headed boy.

'I don't suppose you ever pay your debts, do you?' said Jimmy.

'Sometimes. How's that for a bit on account?'

Before Jimmy could get his guard up, the other's left fist had shot out. It took Jimmy on the mouth. He was off his balance at the moment. Taken by surprise, he staggered and fell.

'Do you want any more?' said the red-haired youth, truculently.

Jimmy got up.

'If you don't mind,' he said quietly, 'I should like a little.'

'Look here,' said one of the group, 'you can't fight here. You'd be stopped in a second. Come behind the gym.'

'Yes, behind the gym. That's the place.'

They all started off in that direction.

'Half a second,' said one of the group, who had not spoken before, a smallish, wiry boy with a pleasant, cheerful face, which Jimmy liked at sight.

'What's up now, Freddy?'

'Only this. It strikes me that it's playing it a bit low down on this chap to hound him into a fight when he comes as an ambassador from another school.'

'My deah chap,' protested Patterne, 'you surely don't call that beastly hole a school?'

Jimmy glared, but, having one fight already on his hands, he refrained from anything in the shape of an active protest. Tommy's cousin's sneer was, however, too much for Ram, whose devotion to Marleigh was almost a religion.

'That,' he said warmly, 'is the crying injustice and beastly shame. For why, Hon'ble Patterne, is our Alma Mater the hole and no school? Do we not sit at the feet of learned masters and drink in jolly stiff lessons? Do not our fathers pay heavily, and through the nose, for us to imbibe the Pierian stream of know-ledge? I bite my thumb at you, young sir.' Here Ram suited the action to the word, to the uproarious delight of the bystanders. 'I am not constitutionally a bellicose, or I would give you the slap in the ear, or the nose-punch. You are an insignificant chap not worth notice.'

'Oh, I am, am I? Well, look heah—'

The boy called Freddy – Frederick Bowdon, to give him his full name – interposed.

'Chuck it, Pat,' he said. 'He's perfectly right. It was a scuggish thing to say, and you ought to apologise. I don't know what you fellows think, but I call it a beastly shame setting on a man from another school like this. He's under a flag of truce. I say,' he added, turning to Jimmy, 'you needn't fight unless you want to, you know. If O'Connell is spoiling for a row, I'll take him on.'

Jimmy could not help laughing at this bright suggestion.

'It's awfully good of you,' he said, 'but don't worry about me. I'm all right.'

'If he funks it—' began O'Connell.

'I don't,' said Jimmy shortly. 'Shall we be going on?'

There was a general movement towards the gymnasium, a grey stone building which lay at the far end of the school grounds. Bowdon came to Jimmy, and walked with him. Other groups of boys whom they met, having inquired what was happening, and learning that it was a fight, joined themselves to the throng, until it became quite a crowd. As they neared the gymnasium, there must have been almost a hundred intending spectators.

'I'm awfully sorry this has happened,' said Bowdon to Jimmy, as they walked along. 'I call it a bally disgrace to the school. An ambassador ought to be safe from this sort of thing. The fact is, the school's in a beastly rotten state just now. O'Connell and his gang seem to think they can do just what they like. I'm about the only fellow, as a matter of fact, who can take on O'Connell, and he keeps clear of me. I'm not saying it from side, you know. I beat him in the light-weight boxing last term. He's a jolly tough nut to crack.'

Jimmy thought he might as well get a few hints as to what sort of a fighter this was whom he was going to meet.

'What's he like? I mean, as a fighter. He looks strong.'

'He is,' said Bowdon, with conviction. 'He's as strong as a horse, and as hard as a block of wood. He hasn't got very much science, luckily. I beat him on points in the boxing. If it had been to a finish, I don't know what might have happened. He was pretty nearly as fresh when we left off as when we started. If I were you, I should keep away from him as much as possible, and especially dodge his right. He's got a tremendous right. I shan't forget one smash in the ribs he got me in the second round, in a hurry. I thought I was out.'

This was not very comforting; but Jimmy had formed much the same opinion of his opponent from the mere sight of him. The red-haired one was evidently plentifully endowed with muscle. A clean hit from him was not likely to be a pleasant experience. Jimmy hoped that his own quickness, which was remarkable, would be sufficient to prevent this. If it did not, it could not be helped. He would fight his best, and he would fight as long as he could stand. If he could not win, he must be content with losing gamely.

'I wish you'd let me second you,' said Bowdon. 'I might be able to give you some tips about him during the fight.'

'I should be awfully glad if you would,' said Jimmy gratefully. 'It's jolly good of you.'

'Not a bit. I hope you'll knock him out. A jolly good licking would do him all the good in the world. Chaps here have begun to look on him as a little tin god.'

'But if you licked him—'

'Oh, they've forgotten that. You see, he bucks about, and behaves as if the place belonged to him, while I lie fairly low.

I never interfere with anybody, if they leave me alone. He sides about like a bally swashbuckler. Here we are. Hullo, here's Williamson, that's good. We'll get him to referee. Then we can be sure of having fair play. He's captain of football here, and was runner-up in the heavy-weights at Aldershot last year. He won't stand any rot from the O'Connell gang.'

A tall, powerful-looking boy had joined the group. He was in football clothes and a blazer. He had been playing fives in one of the courts near the gymnasium.

'Hullo,' he said, 'what's all this?'

A dozen voices started to explain.

'One at a time,' he said. 'What's on, Freddy?'

'It's a fight, Williamson,' said Bowdon, 'between a Marleigh chap – by the way, what's your name? – a Marleigh chap named Stewart—'

'What's a Marleigh chap doing here?'

'He came to see Patterne about the second eleven match.'

'Oh, yes. The second are playing Marleigh instead of the Emeriti. But, look here, this won't do. If fellows from other schools come here, they mustn't be lugged into fights.'

'That's just what I said. But Stewart wants to fight.'

'Who's it with?'

'O'Connell.'

'Oh.'

From his voice it seemed that O'Connell's reputation as a swashbuckler was not unknown to the football captain. He looked with interest at Jimmy.

'Do you really want to fight?'

'Yes,' said Jimmy. 'He hit me. I should like to try and hit him for a change.'

'Oh, all right, then.'

'I say, Williamson,' said Bowdon, 'will you referee?'

'All right, if you want me to. Give us a watch, someone. Thanks. Two-minute rounds, of course, and half a minute in between. Till one of you has had enough. Who's seconding you, Stewart?'

'I am,' said Bowdon.

'That's all right, then. He's lucky as far as that goes. Are you ready?'

Two basins of water and a couple of towels had appeared mysteriously from nowhere. Jimmy and his opponent got ready. A large ring had been formed. O'Connell stepped into it. Jimmy followed him. Two chairs had been brought. Jimmy and O'Connell sat in them, waiting for the call of time.

Jimmy sat in his corner looking at O'Connell on the opposite side of the ring, while Bowdon spoke to Williamson.

He knew he had taken on a big thing, but he had to go through with it; even if he had desired it, there could be no backing out now. It was not that he was afraid, but he felt his heart thumping against his ribs, and wondered if he looked pale or nervous – he hoped not – before that excited crowd, a crowd that was increasing every second. They were not his friends, that was the thought at the back of everything; though they were not actively hostile, they were not his friends, but O'Connell's. To them it was Alderton against Marleigh, and it was their man who must win. Jimmy knew this, and the knowledge did not make him feel any better.

Then he saw Ram standing beside him, and smiled. Ram, looking very woebegone and miserable, gazed vaguely round the ring through his big spectacles as if searching for some friendly face.

Then Bowdon crossed over, and Williamson turned to the crowd.

'You fellows must keep back, understand? And no shouting during the rounds. See. Now, all ready? Wait a bit,' and he looked at his watch. 'Time.'

Jimmy's heart gave an extra big thump, a cold shiver ran down his back, and he drew in a long breath, swallowing with difficulty; but as he advanced to meet O'Connell the nervousness, the dread of the unexpected, left him, and he felt strangely calm, ready for anything.

It was action; action now. No waiting any longer: here was something solid, flesh and blood against him, and, even if he was beaten, he was going to fight for it.

He held out his hand, but O'Connell took no notice, and led at his head quickly. Jimmy side-stepped almost mechanically, and as he did so, found himself saying in his own mind, 'This chap is no gentleman; this is not playing the game,' then he ducked as O'Connell swung his right again.

The Alderton boy meant to finish things quickly, a long fight was not to his taste; his game was to rush, to hit hard and often, and to trust to his strength to pull him through. This Marleigh fellow must be shown that he could not hope to stand up against his betters, and he went at Jimmy, hitting viciously with both hands.

Jimmy gave back a couple of steps and stopped a hard smash at his body, then he countered. He had not realised he had done so, until he felt a sudden unlooked-for jar on the knuckles, and saw a trickle of blood on the other's chin; but he had to give way again, and then his foot slipped on the grass and he went over.

The spectators, forgetting all instructions, yelled, and 'Get back, O'Connell,' shouted Williamson, 'get back,' and to the crowd, 'shut it; that's only a slip.'

Jimmy was up again at once, smash – smash – O'Connell grunted as he bored him to the side, and then, 'Time.'

Ah! that delicious half-minute's rest, lying back in his chair, breathing deeply; while Bowdon flapped him with a towel, and another boy, with a serious brown face and grey eyes, sponged him with refreshing water. Ram, silent till now, turned to the crowd surrounding him.

'This is the strenuous, Misters. This is no mere *casus belli*, but hot stuff.'

'Well done,' said Bowdon, all in a breath, not waiting for an answer, 'keep away from him, right away, out-fighting you know, make him sweat, did that tumble shake you up? You ought to be at school here, oughtn't he, David? Mind his right, and – hullo!'

'Time,' and Jimmy stood up once more.

O'Connell had tried to rush things the first round, he tried even harder in the second, and was on Jimmy like lightning, hitting at him savagely, hustling him all round the ring.

Jimmy, on his side, knew that if once that terrible right got fairly home he was done for; so he kept away, with his left well up, dodging the other's leads as best he could, waiting for the opening he prayed would come. But it was beginning to tell, this fierce sledge-hammer work; O'Connell was far stronger than he was, and was showing it more and more every moment. Then O'Connell dropped his guard slightly, ever so slightly, but it was enough; Jimmy dived in and shook him up with a punch on the body, then in return he went over, rushed off his feet, and time was called.

But Jimmy went to his corner knowing that his man was no boxer, just a plain, straightforward slogger. He could fight, yes; but box, no, not a bit.

The applause at the end of the round was now more evenly divided; Jimmy felt that he was making friends. Had he but known it, the Alderton boys were beginning to feel just a little ashamed of their truculent-looking champion, and the way he had forced this stranger into a fight. Until the two opponents had stood up to each other in their shirt-sleeves, nobody had realised how much slighter Jimmy was, and his plucky stand was making him popular. It had been a joke at first, this fight; now they shuffled uneasily as they watched the Marleigh boy taking his punishment without flinching; and after all, what was the fight about? And then, again – but all the same, Alderton must win.

Jimmy's head was singing, his mouth was bleeding, and his arms felt a bit heavy, but he was still fresh, and breathed easily; while O'Connell opposite, gasped and scowled at his seconds, as they bent over him.

And once more they stood up to fight.

O'Connell, his face marked with purple blotches, his eyes glittering nastily, again led. He knew that this fight he had so eagerly entered on was going to tax his full powers; here was this kid standing up to him still; but this would be the last round, and he rushed, but without the dash of the first two rounds.

Jimmy edged a blow off his body, and then ducked as O'Connell's right whistled past his ear; he countered and felt the crash of his fist against the other's body, and was in again with his right, good blows both, then he found himself struggling in O'Connell's arms.

'Break away,' shouted Williamson, 'break away.' O'Connell's face was white, and he breathed heavily, those two punches were beginning to tell already. Then 'break away, there,' and Jimmy dropped his fists. O'Connell grinned wickedly, and holding him with one hand, lashed out.

Whether it was a foul or not, was always a disputed point at Alderton, and if the truth be known, rather a sore subject for a long time. Williamson, who was on the wrong side to see, thought not; he hesitated to believe that an Alderton fellow could be guilty of hitting while he held an opponent. It is a thing

that no one ever does, and there Williamson left it. And then –
Jimmy was on his back, staring up at the sky, wondering; then
he heard – 'one' – Great Scott; he must get up, he mustn't lie

there – 'two' – he heard Bowdon shouting at Williamson – 'three'
– he was on his hands and knees – 'four' – on one knee – 'five' –
he was keeping his mind firmly fixed on the fact that he must
stand up, if it killed him – 'six' – and 'get back, O'Connell.'
Someone said 'seven' – he was up at last, and O'Connell, white-
faced and hideous, with his mouth open, was on him.

Jimmy had been badly shaken, but the blow had not got him
fairly, or he would not have been on his feet as he was; still he
knew that it would try him hard to get through the rest of the
round. What had he to remember? Oh! yes, that right – and he
fought on in a whirl. Why did not the other finish him off?

He was not hitting very hard; was he staying his hand? And then in a flash came the thought, he couldn't, he couldn't; he was done too, and Jimmy suddenly felt better. 'Time.'

As he turned, a storm of cheers broke out, and Jimmy tottered to his corner, feeling that even if he was an alien, an outlander, somehow he, Jimmy Stewart of Marleigh School, was being cheered by a throng of Alderton fellows, and again he felt better.

Bowdon was flapping him with the towel, sending a perfect current of air into his lungs. That was better – a-ah! – much better, and he breathed deeply. When one is in perfect training as Jimmy was, one can stand a lot of knocking about, and Jimmy felt that that blow of O'Connell's was a mere accident. Whether it was fair or not never troubled him. It would not happen again, he told himself, and his head was better already; after all it was only the sudden shock.

'That,' said a voice, his solemn-faced second's, 'was the most caddish thing I have ever come across. If he had got you fair on—'

'Yes, Williamson was on the off side, but that chap held you as he hit, I swear he did. It's a shame, he ought to have been disqualified. But you hurt him, I think, more than he did you, all the same.'

'Are you feeling all right?'

'Yes, thank you,' said Jimmy, 'my neck's a bit stiff. Otherwise I'm quite fit.'

'Good man.'

'Time!'

O'Connell moved stiffly and with an effort. Jimmy's two body blows in the last round were hurting him.

They circled round each other quietly. O'Connell led at Jimmy's head, but was short, and Jimmy jumped in. O'Connell staggered. Again they moved round, and this time Jimmy led, and O'Connell in his turn got home. But his blows lacked strength. And then Jimmy, from the corner of his eye, saw Bowdon wave his hand. He jumped in again. O'Connell gave way. Jimmy made his big effort. With all the strength that was left in him he went in left and right.

Then suddenly there was nothing to hit at. In a sort of dream he saw that O'Connell was lying on the ground. He stepped back, while Williamson counted the seconds in a solemn voice. O'Connell paid no attention. He was evidently finished. 'Ten,' said Williamson.

Jimmy felt himself gripped by the hand, the centre of a crowd of excited faces. He had beaten their man, but that did not matter. They were sportsmen at Alderton, and they meant to make up for the way in which they had treated this stranger from another school. Everybody was cheering, and slapping Jimmy's back.

'Well played,' said a quiet voice. 'That was ripping.' Jimmy turned and saw Bowdon.

'Thanks awfully for seconding me,' he said.

'Not a bit,' said Bowdon. 'Come and have some tea.'

They made much of Jimmy and Ram in Bowdon's study. Ram was in his element. He made speeches. He drank Jimmy's health in tea. He drank eternal friendship to Bowdon and the others. As a wind-up, by special request, he recited 'The Charge of the Light Brigade.'

'There are the stout fellows and good chaps,' he said enthusiastically to Jimmy, as they started to ride home, turning and waving a hand benevolently to the cheering group at the big gate. 'We came in like lamb, and have gone out like lion and big pot. Huzza! You are the courageous, Hon'ble Stewart.'

Jimmy was feeling too tired for conversation. His head was aching from his exertions. He rode on in silence.

Half-way home he felt a sudden jarring and bumping.

'Dash it, I've punctured,' he said.

He got off.

'You ride on, Ram,' he said. 'I'll stop and patch up this beastly tyre.'

'Shall I not stand by friend in distress?' asked Ram.

'No, thanks. I'd rather be alone. I'm feeling a bit done. I don't want to talk much.'

Ram rode off. Jimmy got out his repairing outfit, and was preparing to take the tyre off, when a spot of rain fell on him, then another. In another moment it was coming down in earnest. Jimmy looked about him for shelter.

A hundred yards away, separated from the road by a field, was a deserted, tumble-down cottage. It was not an inviting-looking spot, but, at any rate, it had a roof. It would at least be drier in there than out on the road. He made a dash for it, wheeling his machine.

'Inside and under shelter,' he chuckled.

'Old Ram'll get soaked,' he said, dabbing at his clothes with his handkerchief. 'Rum old place, this. Shouldn't care to live here, but it's all right to keep out the rain. Hullo! what's that?'

Somebody was coming towards the cottage. At first he thought it might be Ram, returning for shelter. But a voice made itself heard, a man's voice. Jimmy could not distinguish the words, but with a sudden start he recognised the voice. There was no mistaking those deep tones. It was Marshall who was approaching.

There was only one place where Jimmy could hide, and that was the shallow loft, to which a trap-door in the corner of the room gave access. A broken-down ladder led to the trap-door, and Jimmy was on the point of climbing this when he remembered his bicycle. There was no time to hide it securely. The best he could do was to prop it against the wall in the darkest corner of the room – it was all very dark in the cottage, for the windows, which were small, had now, owing to neglect, become completely overgrown with ivy – and fling over it a piece of mildewed sacking which he found on the floor. There was the chance that Marshall, having no reason to suspect his presence, would not think of searching the place.

Having done this, he contrived to mount the rickety ladder and enter the loft just as Marshall and his companion turned in at the door.

The floor of the loft was a sieve of holes. As his eyes grew accustomed to the dark, Jimmy could catch glimpses of the two men. Marshall was smoking a cigar, and the glow lit up his sharp features as he drew in the smoke. The other man Jimmy could not see. He appeared to be sitting down or leaning against one of the walls. At least, he did not walk about, as did Marshall.

The other man spoke. Jimmy had no difficulty in hearing the

words. He seemed to be continuing a conversation which had begun outside the cottage.

'I don't see what you're grumbling about,' he said. 'You've been on worse jobs.'

It was an educated voice – Jimmy could hear that – but not a pleasant one. There was a false smoothness in it which would have put most men on their guard.

'Worse jobs!' said Marshall irritably. Jimmy could see him puffing quickly at his cigar. 'If you mean more dangerous, perhaps I have. It's the infernal difficulty of the thing which is breaking my nerve, Ferris.'

'Dear old boy,' said the man addressed as Ferris, smoothly, 'not quite so free with names, if you don't mind. There's no need for them, and they add a little to the risks of the business, don't you know. See what I mean?'

'Oh, very well,' said Marshall shortly.

'Thought I'd just mention it. Give me a match and proceed. You were talking about the difficulties of this little affair.'

'It is difficult,' said Marshall. 'I've at last succeeded in convincing—'

'Call him Jones,' said Ferris softly, 'or "our employer."'

'Convincing him—'

'"Him" is much better. We'll stick to that.'

'I wish you wouldn't interrupt. I've at last succeeded in convincing him of the difficulties. That is why he sent for you to help. I happened to hear that you were in England, and I mentioned your name to him.'

'These unsolicited tributes to one's merit are very gratifying.'

'I could handle the job alone so long as it was simply a question of Sam Burrows, but now—'

'Well? What now? I don't see your point. Sam was

undoubtedly a tough customer. You have now merely a boy to deal with. I should have thought the thing had simplified itself.'

Marshall uttered an exclamation of impatience.

'You seem to be a perfect fool!' he said sharply.

'These unsolicited tributes are very gratifying,' murmured Ferris.

' "Merely a boy!" "Simplifies itself!" ' Marshall kicked angrily at a fragment of brick on the floor. 'Can't you see that it is not a case of merely a boy? It is a case of a school. Bah! merely a boy! Do you think, if that were all, I should want your help? If young Stewart were at his home I could have the stone in a day. But here! How is one to get at him? He is in a fortress. It is as difficult to get at a boy in his school as it would be to enter a monastery.'

'But – this is very interesting. I have never been brought face to face with our English school system before. Does he never go out of the school grounds?'

'Yes,' said Marshall savagely, 'he does – with a dozen other little brutes hanging on to him like burrs. How can a man do anything? I admit that I am baffled. Perhaps you will be more successful.'

'Perhaps I shall,' said Ferris softly. 'If you will excuse my saying so, my dear old fellow, your methods are excellent in their way, but they have their limitations. At bludgeon work you are capital. But perhaps you lack a certain finesse which I flatter myself I possess. In a case like this I think our mutual friend – er – Jones was wise to call me in. I am not fond of violence – that is more in your line – but it seems to me there is no need for violence here. The affair has passed out of that phase; something a little subtler is needed.'

'We shall be working together,' said Marshall. 'You may try your methods, I shall stick to mine.'

'Dear old boy, you were always so impetuous, weren't you? You would always go blundering straight at the fence. I prefer to walk about and see if I can't find a gate or a gap somewhere. I think the whole business is being conducted on too melodramatic lines. It is a small point, perhaps, but why must our mutual friend arrange this meeting in such an uncommonly damp, dark, beastly spot as this? A far better plan would have been for him to have given us a nice light little lunch at his hotel. Then we could have talked it all over comfortably afterwards over a cigar and coffee. The fact that we shall have deuced bad colds in the head tomorrow does not make our chances of success any brighter. But I suppose, when one is well paid, one must be patient. On the terms on which I am being employed I am prepared to wear a cloak and mask and go about muttering "Aha!" if necessary.'

Marshall made no reply, but continued to pace up and down. Jimmy saw him light a second cigar.

Ferris began to speak again.

'I suppose,' he said reflectively, 'it is the privilege of the employer to be unpunctual at the rendezvous, but I wish our friend Jones would not exercise it so rigorously. We were instructed to be here at half-past five. It is now nearly ten minutes to six, but I see no signs of him.'

'Perhaps the rain has stopped him,' growled Marshall. 'Hark! was that a footstep?' Ferris listened. Jimmy, up in the loft, could hear that somebody was walking towards the cottage. The footsteps had a curiously irregular sound.

A moment later a small figure was silhouetted against the light of the open door. Jimmy could not see him clearly enough to judge of his appearance, but he saw that he was lame. One of his legs was shorter than the other.

'Marshall!' said the newcomer in a sharp voice of authority.

'Here, sir.' A note of respect had come into Marshall's voice which had been markedly absent before.

'Ferris.'

'Here I am,' came Ferris's smooth voice. 'Ready, aye, ready, as Nelson or somebody observed.'

The lame man turned to Marshall.

'Well?' he said.

'I am afraid that I was unsuccessful, sir.'

The lame man uttered a guttural exclamation of annoyance. From his voice he seemed to be a foreigner. There was nothing English about his accent.

'Explain,' he said.

'I went to the school,' said Marshall, 'and saw the boy, but it was useless. Somehow – how I cannot explain – he had got wind of my fight with Burrows in the study that night. How he knew that I was the man I cannot tell. He cannot have been in the room.'

'Why?'

'I should have seen him. There was nowhere for him to hide.'

The lame man's voice, when he spoke, was quivering with suppressed anger.

'You would have seen him, would you, Marshall? You use your eyes well, Marshall? Is that so? Fool! Did you see anything as you came to this cottage?'

'No, sir.' Marshall's voice was sullen.

'You did not see footprints in the mud? No, your good eyes did not see those. Nor the track of a bicycle in the mud? No, your keen eyes overlooked that. I saw them, Marshall. Yes, and I saw that on no side of the cottage was there in the mud the track of a bicycle going away or footprints coming away. Yes, Marshall.'

Jimmy's heart gave a great leap. Marshall sprang forward.

'You mean—'

'The boy is here, in this cottage, hiding. You will say: Why the boy? Why not any ordinary cyclist? Bah! why should an ordinary cyclist hide? This boy must have been in the cottage when you arrived. He heard your voice – you would have been speaking. You speak too much – and he hid.'

'Dear old boy,' murmured Ferris, 'you have been a little indiscreet, I fear.'

The lame man peered round him. Jimmy could see his eyes shining in the dark like a cat's. Suddenly he made an ungainly dash forward.

'See!' he hissed. 'See, see! Look at it, Marshall. Can you see it? What is this?'

'It looks uncommonly like a boy's bicycle,' drawled Ferris. 'Dear me! how sad that one so young should practise deceit! Excuse me, sir, but that ladder—'

The lame man turned his eyes in the direction indicated. Then he laughed softly.

'Marshall,' he said, 'climb that ladder, if you please, and ask our young friend to be good enough to join us.'

Marshall looked up. To all appearances the trap-door hadn't been disturbed for weeks. He was about to remark this, but thought better of it. Silently he mounted the ladder, and slowly made his way upward.

The others watched him eagerly.

It is probable that many boys in Jimmy's place would have recognised that the game was up, and, realising this, would have thrown up the sponge and gone down the ladder without further delay. But Jimmy came of a fighting stock. He had not the slightest intention of surrendering without a struggle. He would just as soon have given in to O'Connell in the fight an hour back. Jimmy was his father in miniature, with his father's traditions, just as his father was the British Army in miniature, with its traditions. The British Army generally puts up something of a fight when the moment arrives, and that spirit was a second nature to Colonel Stewart and to Jimmy himself. Where another boy might have lifted the trap-door and climbed down the ladder, Jimmy, looking about him for a weapon, waited for Marshall to lift it and climb up.

The weapon was ready to his hand in an unwieldy piece of wood which had once formed part of the flooring. It was almost separated from the other planks, joined to them only by a few rusty nails, and it came away silently in Jimmy's hand.

He lifted it and waited.

He could hear Marshall fumbling with the trap-door. Presently, with a slight creaking, it rose. Marshall's head appeared in the opening. And at that instant Jimmy struck at it with his plank.

Struck is hardly, perhaps, the word, for the plank was too heavy and unwieldy to use as a club. But he half struck with it and half let it fall, just as Marshall's head and shoulders entered the loft.

At the last moment the latter saw the danger, and attempted to draw back. But it was too late. He succeeded in avoiding the full force of the blow, but the plank struck him slantingly on the side of the head, and fell with a crash on to the floor of the loft, while Marshall dropped back with a groan, the trap-door shutting with a bang behind him. Jimmy heard the thud as he fell to the ground, and then for a moment there was absolute stillness. The unexpectedness of the disaster had silenced the enemy.

Presently Jimmy heard whispers, then another groan. Then Ferris's voice saying, 'He's all right. He's coming to.'

He waited breathlessly for the next move.

Apparently the enemy were considering the position. This unexpected resistance had taken them by surprise. He heard whisperings.

Then Ferris's voice hailed him.

'Mr Stewart.'

'Well?' said Jimmy, after a momentary pause.

'Don't you think, my boy, that you had better come down without any of this fuss? You are giving a great deal of unnecessary trouble.'

There was something about this shouted conversation which appealed to Jimmy's sense of humour even in that crisis. The most imminent danger has not the power to stifle one's sense of the ridiculous, and Jimmy could not help being reminded of a ventriloquial entertainment which he had once heard, where the performer had carried on a conversation with an acquaintance on the roof of the hall.

'I'm quite comfortable where I am, thanks,' said Jimmy.

'I'm advising you for your own good,' said the smooth voice from below.

'Thanks,' said Jimmy drily.

'We're bound to get you. It's only a question of time. And the more trouble you give, the worse it will be for you in the end.'

Jimmy made no reply to this. It was an aspect of the affair of which he preferred not to think too much. He liked to fix his mind on the fact that they had not got him yet, and that, all things considered, he was in a fairly strong position. As far as he could see, the only means of entrance to the loft was by way of the trap-door; and he felt himself capable of guarding that all night. Indeed, he rather hoped that another attack would be made from that quarter. His blood was up now, and he would have welcomed another chance of active fighting.

Below there was a stir. Evidently Marshall had recovered, and was on his feet again. Jimmy could hear him swearing faintly.

'Have a pull at this,' said Ferris.

A flask apparently changed hands. He heard Marshall utter a deep satisfied 'Ah-ah!'

'*That's* the stuff,' said Ferris. 'I think I'll try a little drop myself. Mr Stewart,' he called.

'Well?' said Jimmy.

'I am drinking to our speedy acquaintance.'

'Thanks,' said Jimmy. 'If you'll step up that ladder and open the trap-door, you'll find me here.'

Marshall's voice broke in, thick and furious.

'You young whelp! I'll pay you for this! I'll—' He burst into a flood of threats.

'I'm afraid you have annoyed our friend here, Mr Stewart,' said Ferris blandly. 'He is quite cross.'

All this while the lame man had made no sound, but now he began to speak rapidly in a language which was strange to Jimmy. He spoke in quick, sharp sentences. It seemed to Jimmy that he was giving advice or orders. When he stopped, Ferris said, 'Not at all a bad idea. I had thought of something of the kind myself.'

The next thing that happened took Jimmy completely by surprise. Suddenly, as he stood listening, there was a sound like a very soft cough, and simultaneously something ripped through the floor a yard from where he stood and passed through the thatched roof. The next moment the same thing happened again. Then he understood. It was the air-gun, that quiet, deadly weapon which had struck down Sam Burrows in the drive at home on the night when he had first made the acquaintance of the blue stone.

He crouched back against the wall as a third shot smashed through the floor.

Even as he did so he thought that the attackers must be nearly at the end of their tether if they had to try desperate measures like this. It must mean that they had given up all hope of storming the loft, and were trusting to the chance of maiming him with a random shot.

There did not seem to be much danger of this happening. The shots were passing through the floor several feet from where he stood. After the first shock of the surprise he began to smile again. It was a foolish thing to do, this shooting. While it continued it meant that he was safe as far as a direct assault went. He leaned against the wall and waited.

Presently the shots ceased. In the room below there was complete silence.

A few minutes later a curious sound broke the stillness. At first

Jimmy could not locate it. Then it flashed on him what it was, and all his feeling of confidence left him.

Somebody was tearing away the thatched roof.

Jimmy's position was now becoming desperate. He had not reckoned on an attack from above, and it chilled him to think how helpless he was against such a move. His good plank was useless now. That very heaviness and unwieldiness which made it so excellent a weapon against an attack from below rendered it useless now. He could barely lift it, much less handle it as a club. He must trust to his hands. And what sort of a fight could he make with them against a grown man? And if he could manage him, how could he guard the trap-door and prevent the others coming up from below? For the first time he felt like giving up the struggle.

The man on the roof was digging like a dog at a rabbit-hole. The sodden thatch, once the first layer had been removed, offered little resistance. Jimmy could hear it being torn away in great handfuls. Presently a glimpse of daylight appeared, and the gap widened swiftly. Now Jimmy could see a head and shoulders. He stood rigid, unable to move.

A soft voice from above addressed him.

'I shall not keep you waiting very much longer, Mr Stewart,' said Ferris.

And almost at the same instant he sprang down into the loft.

What happened then had all the suddenness and unexpectedness of a dream. Jimmy saw Ferris spring, heard the crash of his feet on the floor, and then the air was filled with noise and dust, and he was looking down into a ragged gap. The planks, rotten with age and damp, had been unable to bear the shock, and had given way, taking Ferris with them. Jimmy had a momentary sight of the latter seated in the midst of a heap of debris with a dazed look on his face, and leaned back against the wall, shaking with hysterical laughter.

The sound seemed to madden Ferris. His smoothness and humorous calm vanished. He sprang to his feet with a curse.

'Give me that gun, Marshall,' he cried furiously.

Jimmy darted to one side as a shot splashed against the wall where he had been standing.

He was on the alert for another, but it did not come. He heard the lame man say something sharply in his strange tongue. The other seemed to listen. Another word from the lame man, and they had left the cottage. Jimmy heard them scrambling out of the window at the back of the room, bursting through the ivy with furious haste.

He was wondering if this were a fresh development of the attack when the sound of voices came to his ears.

'Here you are, Jim. This way to the Court of Honour.'

'All change for the Scenic Railway.'

'I'm not half soaked, I *don't* think.'

'Come along, Ada. Make yourself at home.'

Jimmy moved so as to get a sight of the door. A party of cyclists ran in, wheeling their machines. Their voices were not naturally harmonious, but to Jimmy at that moment they sounded like the sweetest music.

He was safe.

He opened the trap-door and climbed down the ladder.

' 'Ullo! 'ullo! 'ullo!' said one of the party. 'See what's come down the chimney. What ho! Santa Claus!'

'Beastly wet, isn't it?' said Jimmy. 'I came in here for shelter. I've been exploring.'

The cyclists were a friendly band. They made Jimmy one of themselves. They sang music-hall songs with great cheerfulness, and cracked small jokes, till one of the party, stationed at the door, announced that the rain had stopped, and that they might as well be popping off. Jimmy walked to the road with them, and they parted with expressions of mutual esteem. They were going in the direction from which Jimmy had come. He wheeled his bicycle on towards the school. He felt curiously dazed, as if he had wakened.

Half a mile from the cottage the road passed through an avenue of trees.

As Jimmy entered this avenue a man stepped out into the road in front of him, a tall man with a bandaged head. At first Jimmy took him for a tramp. It was not till he spoke that he realised that he was face to face with Marshall once more.

Ram meanwhile, full of triumph at the victory which had attended the Marleigh arms, as represented by Jimmy, the fighter, and, in a lesser but still glorious degree, by himself, the friend, looker-on, and sympathiser, had ridden on to tell the great news to the school. It was a proud moment for Ram. As he had frequently observed, he was not by nature a temerarious, and he glowed at the thought of the great victory with which he had been connected. It was true that he had not actually fought – it was Jimmy who had done that – but he had stood by and represented Marleigh among the spectators.

'Huzza!' shouted Ram as he rode.

He would probably have gone on shouting 'Huzza!' all the way back in a sort of chant, varied by excited exclamations in the language of his fathers – he was apt to drop into Hindustani when moved – but after he had gone about a mile on his way the storm broke.

Ram hated rain, and this was particularly rainy rain. It sluiced down from the grey sky like water from a shower-bath. His clothes were soaked before he had travelled a hundred yards. His gold spectacles were moist and clouded. He could barely see.

It was this that proved his undoing. Pedalling damply along, he did not notice a sharp bend in the road. For one moment he proceeded unsteadily along the damp grass at the roadside, then shot like an arrow into the ditch, his bicycle clattering behind him.

There was a good deal of water in the ditch, but on the whole mud was the leading feature of its contents. Ram literally wallowed in it. When he sat up and crawled painfully out, he was caked from head to foot, a very different person from the Ram who had shouted 'Huzza!' five minutes before.

'This,' he said to himself as he picked up his machine, 'is the pretty kettle of fish!'

The kettle of fish was even prettier, on a close examination, than he had suspected. As he picked up his bicycle and started to wheel it out into the road, he saw that something was wrong with it.

To Ram there were only two sorts of bicycles: the bicycle that was all right and the bicycle that had something wrong with it. He knew no degrees in the latter class. It was only with the greatest difficulty, and more pain than he had ever endured in any other way, that he had succeeded in actually learning to ride. He had never aspired to the understanding and repairing of bicycles. As a matter of fact, all that was wrong with his machine could have been put right with a spanner in five minutes; but, as far as Ram was concerned, the thing was a wreck.

In this crisis he thought of Jimmy. Hon'ble Stewart, as he knew well, had an almost uncanny familiarity with the workings of bicycles. He would retrace his steps, meet Hon'ble Stewart, and put the case in his hands.

So Ram proceeded to wheel his machine disconsolately back along the road. Soon after this the rain, as if satisfied with what it had done, stopped; and Ram, having wiped his spectacles, was now more in a position to see things.

He trudged on.

\* \* \*

Jimmy stopped and faced Marshall with a sinking heart. The road was deserted. His cyclist friends were miles away by this time. If only he had stopped to mend his puncture before going on! Then he might have swerved past Marshall and ridden on to safety. But in his eagerness to get away from the cottage at the earliest possible moment he had postponed the repairs; and now he was trapped again, as surely as he had been in the cottage a quarter of an hour ago.

'Well, my young friend,' said Marshall, 'so we resume our interrupted conversation. We can talk at our leisure now, which is so much pleasanter, is it not? You will think me a bore, I am afraid, to keep harping on the same subject, but I must ask you once more for that stone.'

'I haven't got it,' said Jimmy. 'I told you so before.'

'So you did, so you did. And yet, somehow, I can't help feeling that you were mistaken. Out with it, if you please. At once.'

'I tell you—' began Jimmy.

'Very well,' said Marshall between his teeth, 'if you stick to it.'

He made a step towards Jimmy. Jimmy backed. His bicycle was still between them, and that checked the other for the moment. But only for a moment. Springing forward, Marshall had seized him by the arm in a grip of steel, when a polite voice from behind his back made him drop Jimmy and spin round.

'Excuse the complete stranger, Hon'ble sir,' said the voice, 'but are you by chance the skilled mechanic? I have here a bicycle—'

'Ram!' shouted Jimmy, with a sudden rush of relief.

'Hon'ble Stewart! I did not suspect that you, too, were among those present. This is the glad meeting.'

An idea flashed across Jimmy's mind.

'This way, you chaps!' he shouted. 'Here I am!'

Marshall, who had been standing as if undecided what to do, waited no longer. With a muttered oath he slipped back through the hedge, and began to run across the field into the gathering dusk. They could hear his footsteps squelching across the damp turf. The advent of Ram had unnerved him, and Jimmy's words had completed the effect. He saw in Ram the advance-guard of a body of Jimmy's schoolfellows, a notion which Jimmy's shout had confirmed. To attempt to regain the stone from Jimmy forcibly before witnesses was more than even he dared.

'By Jove! Ram,' said Jimmy, 'I'm glad you turned up.'

Ram was looking wonderingly in the direction in which Marshall had vanished.

'What,' he asked, 'was the matter with the mister? Why did he run like hare and vanish like snow before rays of sun?'

'I expect he couldn't stand your handsome face, Ram,' said Jimmy with a grin. 'I find it jolly difficult sometimes myself.'

'What was it that you and he were having snip-snap and *sotto-voce* conversation about? Was he chum or chance acquaintance?'

'Bit of both, I should call him. Come on, Ram, we must run.'

'Run?' repeated Ram vaguely.

'Yes, *run*, you rotter. Run like hares and vanish like snow before rays of sun. See?'

'But my bicycle?'

'Dash your bike! What's up with it? Never mind, I'll mend it in half a jiffy. Only we must get away from here at once. He may be coming back. We'll run on about a quarter of a mile. Then we can stop and do repairs. Come on; don't stand there looking like a golliwog! Run, man, *run!*'

And Ram ran, marvelling.

The afternoon of the great concert had arrived. For days Tommy Armstrong had been rushing round, beating up talent with all the persuasiveness at his command, which was considerable. Herr Steingruber's amiability had been more pronounced every time he met his class, and it was rumoured that he sat up till unheard-of hours practising on his 'cello, to the marked discomfort of his next-door neighbours, who were soulless people who wanted sleep. Bills had been written out by Tommy and his friends in a fair, round hand-writing, setting forth the outlines of the treat that might be expected, and mentioning that the concert was 'for a deserving object.' That was as far as the impresarios dared to go in the way of writing, but Tommy, questioned by interested members of the school on the subject, had spread the news that the deserving object was the Spinder's House Food Fund; and the school, approving of the cause, had promised to roll up. Binns and Sloper practised duets daily, and the brothers Tooth had the comfortable feeling, when they embarked on their usual morning fight, that they were killing two birds with one stone, working off their grievances and also rehearsing for their boxing exhibition.

'It'll be quite a pleasant change for them, sparring with the gloves on,' said Tommy reflectively, as he watched the great twin brethren joining battle. 'Quite refreshing for 'em.'

Herr Steingruber drew Tommy aside one morning. 'In der virst bart of der brogramme, my liddle Armsdrong,' he said beamingly, 'I shall der Moonlight Zonada of Beethoven blay. In der zecond bart – zo – a liddle dthing of my own gombosition I vill for der virst dime on dis or any odder sdage berform. He is a – what you say? – a zort of vairy legend of Shermany which I have in my youth ad Heidelberg heard and jodded down; und now I him zet to musig and do you and do der odder liddle vellows now for der virst dime blay. Jah, zo.'

'That'll be ripping, sir,' said Tommy doubtfully.

'Jah, zo. Ribbing. Dot vos him. You und der odders, you will glap your hands und say, "Goot! Dot vos goot!"'

'Of course we shall, sir,' said Tommy. 'But – er – I suppose you don't know any cake-walks, do you sir?'

'Gayg-walks, my liddle vellow?'

'Yes, sir. "Smoky Mokes" or "Bill Simmons," or something like that.'

'Jah, I onderstand. I know der "Pill Zimmons." But he is not der goot musig, my Armsdrong.'

'It's a ripping tune, sir. I'm sure the chaps would like it.'

'Ah, no, no, Armsdrong. He vos der bad, light musig.'

And Tommy had been able to draw no other opinion from him.

The gymnasium was crowded when the time arrived for the curtain to go up. Most of the audience had been there for a quarter of an hour or more, and there was a general demand that the thing should start. Everybody, in fact, was ready for the curtain to go up, except the curtain, which absolutely declined to oblige.

This curtain was a sheet which Tommy had draped with great skill in front of the improvised platform. It was supposed to roll up when Thomson, stationed there for the purpose, hauled on a rope. All that happened, however, when Thomson pulled, was that the rope broke.

A chorus of advice and abuse came from every part of the room. Tommy rose to the situation like a Napoleon. He caught hold of the sheet and put all his weight into one tug. The sheet came away with a rending sound, amidst roars of applause, leaving the platform open to the public view, with the piano in one corner and Stephens Tertius, in his shirt-sleeves, adjusting his braces, in the centre. It had occurred to Stephens Tertius that his trousers were braced a shade too high, and he hoped to be able to put the matter right before the curtain rose.

Tommy, in his role of announcer, flung away the sheet and stepped to the front.

'Order, please,' he yelled. 'Jellicoe, I'll come down and kick you in a second. Ladies and gentlemen, item one on the programme. Song, "Annie Laurie," Mr Stephens Tertius.'

'Half a second,' growled the songster; 'let a chap finish dressing first.'

'No, go on,' hissed Tommy. 'There'll be a row if you don't start.'

He did start, and yet there was a row, Stephens Tertius's voice was in that uncomfortable state when a voice is not quite certain whether it is a treble or a bass. It tries both at intervals, as if anxious to make up its mind.

Stephens Tertius started 'Annie Laurie' in about as high a key as a human being could achieve. He got through the first line without a hitch.

As he began line two a small, austere voice from the back of the room spoke.

'Your bags are coming down, Stephens,' said the voice dispassionately.

Stephens started as one who has had bad news from home,

and his voice, seizing the opportunity now that his attention was off it, suddenly changed to the deepest bass. A thrill of excitement ran through the audience, a sort of startled gasp, and then a roar of applause rent the air. Stephens sang on to the end of the verse, quite inaudible, and then backed off the platform, crimson in the face, refusing to return in spite of a loud encore.

Tommy stepped to the front again.

'Order, please,' he shouted. 'Item two on the programme. Penny whistle solo, "Poppies," by Mr J. Cheetham.'

This, one is sorry to have to record, proved a complete frost. Certain frivolous spirits in the first row, who had come expecting some such turn as this, produced lemons from their pockets, and began to suck them in an ostentatious manner, which soon had its effect on the unfortunate performer on the penny whistle. Cheetham watched the operation with fearful scowls for some bars. Then the flow of music gradually dwindled away, ending in a sickly note like the chirp of some newly-born bird. Tommy hustled the indignant penny-whistler off the stage, listening unmoved to his complaints and threats of what he would do to the lemon-suckers when he met them outside.

The next item on the programme should by right have been Herr Steingruber's 'cello solo, but the first two turns had caved in so badly that Tommy did not dare to risk another failure. He postponed the Herr's performance, and put on what he knew was bound to be a success, the inter-Tooth boxing competition.

A lifetime devoted to fighting each other had given the Tooth twins a certain skill with their hands, which, added to their great natural energy, made their warfare highly popular in the school.

'Gentlemen,' said Tommy, 'the next turn will be a three-round boxing exhibition, Queensberry rules, by the brothers Tooth. I must request kind friends in front to abstain from applause during the rounds, and if young Sickers at the end of the fifth row doesn't stop chucking nutshells about I'll come down and punch his ugly head till his teeth rattle. Are you ready? Time!'

The two pugilists wasted no time sparring. They charged in at each other with a willingness greatly to the taste of the audience, who, ignoring Tommy's request for silence during the rounds, yelled and whistled all the time.

The round ended in one of the combatants making a furious rush at his opponent, who dodged, with the result that the former flew off the platform into the front seats, to the huge delight of everybody except the occupants of those seats. As these were the very scoundrels who had sucked lemons during his turn, Cheetham was especially pleased, and began to think that there was such a thing as poetic justice in the world after all.

The next two rounds, though less sensational, were extremely brisk; and the audience were in a thoroughly good humour at the call of time. Tommy congratulated himself on his foresight in altering the order of the turns. The Tooth brethren had ensured the success of the entertainment.

When Herr Steingruber mounted the dais the cheering was inclined to be ironical. The German master looked round the room with a benevolent smile.

'My liddle vriendts,' he said, 'I vill a gombosition dot do you familiar possibly may be endeavour to berform. My vriendt Dollervield will mit der aggombaniment on der biano assisd.'

Tollerfield was a tall boy with a grave face and spectacles. Nobody knew much about him except that he played the piano very well. Tommy, as he watched the solemnity with which the accompanist struck a few preliminary chords, feared the worst. He began to regret that he had asked Herr Steingruber to perform at all. How would the chaps take it? Would they put up with some long classical composition which they could not understand and did not want to? It was a pity that this should happen just when the concert was beginning to go with such a swing.

Tollerfield played a very slow, mournful prelude, and the 'cello moved into a soft, at first almost inaudible, melody. At first Tommy did not recognise it, but suddenly it quickened and swelled, and he gasped with relief. The Herr was playing 'Bill Simmons.'

The audience uttered a suppressed yell of joy. Feet began to tap in time to the music. Herr Steingruber increased the pace. His bow flew over the strings. He finished with a deep, long-drawn note, rose, and bowed. The house rose at him. There was a universal demand for an encore. The Herr, beaming proudly, obliged. As he stepped down from the platform Tommy approached him, almost tearful with relief.

'That was ripping, sir,' he said warmly. 'It was awfully good of you to play. It'll be the best thing on the programme by miles.'

Herr Steingruber beamed.

'Ach, my liddle Armsdrong,' he said, 'I did dthink id over do myself, und I do der gonglusion gom dot id would be better dan der grand of Beethoven musig. Id is best vor us der dastes of der audience do sdudy, zo! In der zegond bart of der brogramme I vill der "Smogy Moges" blay. Zo!'

Tommy's last anxiety was relieved. Now the entertainment was bound to go.

Binns and Sloper followed with a duet, after which Morrison gave what he called imitations of famous music-hall artistes. In each of these he was more like himself than ever, but the audience were not in the mood to be too critical now, and, as they knew the tunes of the songs Morrison sang and could join in the choruses, they asked no more. They simply sat tight and made the place rock.

In the second half of the programme the star turn was undoubtedly Ram's recitation of Hamlet's soliloquy. Even in its original form this is admitted by most people to be a pretty good piece of writing, and Ram improved on the original. He happened to forget the exact words half-way through, and, scorning to retire gracefully, as a lesser man might have done, he improvised. It was felt that Shakespeare would have been glad if he had known.

'Smoky Mokes' proved as great a success as 'Bill Simmons' had done, and Herr Steingruber, having played an encore, left the hall feeling quietly contented. It was the object of his life to get into closer touch with the boys of the school, and there was no doubt that tonight he had made a big step in that direction. The feeling in the school was one of vague surprise that they could have failed to appreciate the German master at his full value till now. Men who could play 'Smoky Mokes' on the 'cello were deserving of respect.

At the conclusion of the final turn Tommy stepped on to the platform to say a few words.

'I hope you fellows enjoyed the show,' he said when he could make himself heard. 'It was jolly good of you to roll up. I can tell you we want the money badly. You've no notion of the muck Spinder makes us eat. We all felt it was about time something was done. I think all present who have had anything to do with it will agree with me that the meals at Spinder's are about as near the limit as − as, well, as anything can—'

He broke off. Not because he had finished what he had to say. Indeed, he had only just begun, and could have spoken at some length on what was his favourite subject. The reason why he stopped was because he happened to see that the audience had increased by one since he opened his remarks, and that that one was Mr Spinder himself.

'Pray continue, Armstrong,' said Mr Spinder coldly.

'I – er – I think that's about all, sir,' said the unfortunate Tommy.

'I should like to see you in my room, Armstrong.'

'Yes, sir.'

Mr Spinder left the gymnasium, while Tommy, jumping down from the platform, prepared to follow. How much had the master heard? That was what he wanted to know. Of course, there was bound to be a row about this food business sooner or later when it came to a head; but he did not want it to come to a head prematurely. Nor was he particularly anxious to appear too prominently as the leader of the movement.

He made inquiries of the audience. Nobody seemed to know exactly how long Mr Spinder had been standing at the door.

'Oh, well,' said Tommy, philosophically, 'I suppose I shall soon know.'

Mr Spinder was walking up and down his room when he arrived. He turned sharply on Tommy.

'I wish to know what all this nonsense is about, Armstrong,' he said brusquely.

'Sir?' said Tommy, to gain time.

'You know what I mean.'

'It's about the food, sir.'

Mr Spinder's eyes glowed.

'Once and for all, Armstrong,' he said, 'there must be an end of this.'

'An end!' thought Tommy. 'Great Scott! It's only just beginning!'

'I have had to speak to you about this before. You seem to be the chief mover in a kind of foolish agitation which is going on in my house. I tell you, Armstrong, I will not have it. There is a certain type of boy who delights in promoting strife of all kinds in a school. You are a boy of that sort. You will learn that it does not pay. If I have any more of this absurd conduct, I shall punish you very heavily. Very heavily indeed. What was all that nonsense you were saying tonight?'

'I was making one or two remarks, sir,' said Tommy, diffidently. One wanted supporters for a job of this kind. If he had been at the head of a deputation he would have been boldness itself; but somehow he could not help feeling very lonesome, all by himself in the study.

'Yes,' said Mr Spinder, growing gradually more angry, 'I heard you, I heard you. You were speaking in an extremely impertinent and disrespectful manner.'

'Whew!' murmured Tommy to himself, surreptitiously mopping his forehead. The pace was getting too warm for him.

'I— Who's that? Come in.'

The handle turned. The form of Morrison appeared.

'Well, Morrison, what is it?' snapped Mr Spinder. He hated being interrupted.

'Please, sir, may I have a plain-ruled exercise-book?'

A hasty consultation among the members of Mr Spinder's house – Tommy's immediate circle of friends, that is to say – had resulted in a decision to act for the latter's good, as far as in them lay. There was Tommy in the hands of the enemy. It was their duty to see that he was not handled too roughly. So they proceeded to act on the lines adopted by Spanish bull-fighters, whose plan it is to distract the attention of the bull from their comrade by means of small side-attacks.

'Exercise-book?' said Mr Spinder, irritably. 'What in the world do you want with an exercise-book now?'

'Only in case I should happen to want it tomorrow morning, sir,' said Morrison, whose powers of impromptu invention were unequal to the tax so suddenly laid upon them.

'You come here and interrupt me when I am talking to Armstrong, and waste my time with foolish— Go away, Morrison; and do me a hundred lines,' thundered the master.

'Yes, sir,' said Morrison, meekly, as he withdrew.

Mr Spinder turned to Tommy again.

'I have been watching you for some time, I may tell you, Armstrong. I have had my eye on you. You are a thoroughly undisciplined and disorderly boy. I shall take no notice of your absurd complaints about the food, which is perfectly good, except to punish you very severely if you are foolish enough to repeat them. I tell you I will not— Come in!' He broke off with increased irritation, and watched the door angrily through his spectacles.

The door opened, and the mildly beaming face of Ram loomed into view.

'Well? Well? Well?' Mr Spinder's voice was tense with suppressed annoyance.

Ram cleared his throat nervously. He was not liking this job, but he meant to go through with it courageously.

'Hon'ble Spinder,' he began.

'Don't call me "Hon'ble Spinder." I have spoken to you of this before. You are at an English school, so be good enough to conform to our English school customs. Call me "sir" when you speak to me, if you please. Well, what is it?'

'Distinguished sir—'

Mr Spinder stamped. Then, as if feeling that the sooner he heard what Ram had to say the sooner he would be able to resume his remarks to Tommy, he restrained himself and said, 'Well?'

'Distinguished sir—'

A look of pain and agitation passed over Ram's face. With a sinking sensation in his interior he realised that he had forgotten the message which his friends had arranged for him to speak. In his agitation he could only remember the one which Morrison had selected.

'Distinguished sir,' he stammered, 'do not look on me as the unwelcome visitor and beastly bore. May I be conceded a plain-ruled exercise-book?'

Mr Spinder's restraint disappeared. He gesticulated silently for a while, then pointed to the door.

'Two hundred lines,' he cried, furiously, 'for gross impertinence. Two hundred lines. Go, go.'

Ram went.

The master took a turn up and down the room to recover himself. He was about to attack Tommy once more, when there was a third knock at the door.

This time Mr Spinder did not wait for the visitor to turn the handle. He rushed to the door with a sort of choked cry and flung it open.

On the mat outside stood the headmaster's butler regarding him with a stolid stare.

You cannot give a butler two hundred lines for knocking at your door. Nor can you shout at him to tell you why he has come.

Mr Spinder controlled his voice sufficiently to ask more or less mildly what was the occasion of the visit. The butler handed him a note.

'From the headmaster, sir.'

Mr Spinder read its contents.

'Wait here,' he said to Tommy. 'I shall return in a moment.'

And he left the room, closing the door behind him.

When he was alone Tommy's mind worked quickly. More than anything else, he wanted to see what it was that Mr Spinder kept concealed behind the books on his bookshelf. It must be something of a value out of the common run to lead to two men breaking into the house and searching the room, as they had done on the night when he and Jimmy had hid behind the piano.

He had marked down the particular shelf that night from his hiding-place. It only remained to discover the exact book which Mr Spinder had taken from the shelf. As he had looked from behind the piano, he had fancied that it was one of the first ten or so from the right. It had been hard to see clearly. Now there was a chance to find out for certain.

It was best to do the thing thoroughly. He removed the first book. There was nothing behind it but the mahogany of the shelf. He replaced it, and drew out the second. Again no result. The third and forth yielded nothing.

'Never mind,' said Tommy; 'I know I'm on the track.'

In the cavity left by the fifth volume he came on the first proof of this statement. Between the shelf and the back wall of wood there was a distinct crevice. It seemed to Tommy to widen as it ran along the shelf. With an eager exclamation he drew out the sixth book.

Yes! the crevice had widened considerably. It had now become large enough for him to insert the first joint of his finger.

What was there behind the seventh book, a ponderous volume on Oriental mythology? He tore it from its place, and plunged his hand into the opening. His fingers struck on something small and hard, something that felt like a small nut.

'Got him!' said Tommy, joyfully.

He was pulling it out when the tread of feet in the corridor came to him. The removal and replacing of the books had taken time. Each volume was large and awkward to handle. He had only just time to push the 'Oriental Mythology' back into its place and leap away from the shelf when the door opened and Mr Spinder re-entered.

The headmaster had been consulting Mr Spinder on matters connected with the work of the school, and his mind was too full of this when he returned to allow him leisure for concentrating himself on Tommy. He dealt with him briefly, by giving him three hundred lines, and then dismissed him.

Tommy walked away from the study thoughtfully. 'Seventh book from the end of the shelf,' he murmured to himself. 'I must remember that. I wonder what that thing was? And I wonder when I shall get another chance of looking? Beastly bad luck being interrupted just as I had tracked the thing down.'

It was while Tommy was working off his three hundred lines in the dayroom next morning before school that he was aware of a rising argument between the Teeth. As a rule he was quite glad to sit and watch the twins brawling, but just at present he had work to do, and their voices disturbed him. So, throwing a dictionary at the nearest twin by way of a protest, he inquired what the dickens the matter was. In a moment the Teeth were at his side, voluble and explanatory.

'Oh, give us a chance,' said Tommy, putting his hands to his ears. 'One at a time, one at a time.'

Gradually the cause of strife made itself clear. It seemed that one of the brothers was accusing the other of bagging an ivory penholder from his play-box. The second brother stoutly denied this.

'Well, you're the only chap who's got a key that fits my box. You know they were bought at the same shop, and the locks are just the same.'

'All the same, I didn't bag your beastly pen. I wouldn't touch it with a barge-pole.'

'Give it up.'

'All right, then, call me a liar.'

'All right, I will, then.'

'Do you think I bagged your beastly pen?'

'Yes, I do think you bagged my pen.'

Tommy intervened.

'My dear young friends,' he said, 'at any other time I should be delighted to listen to your bright and interesting conversation; but just at present I happen to be doing three hundred lines for that blighter Spinder against time, so I should be glad if you would finish your argument about half a mile away. Otherwise I shall be reluctantly compelled to knock your ugly little heads together.'

The twins departed, and Tommy, full of unkind thoughts about Mr Spinder, resumed his imposition.

That was the first hint Tommy got that something was wrong in the house. When, later in the morning, Morrison came to him with the statement that a leather ink-pot had disappeared from his play-box, Tommy wondered a little at the coincidence, but nothing more. It was not till Bellamy, his customary calm laid aside, went about complaining in an agitated voice that two pounds of mixed chocolates had gone from his box that the thing really became sinister.

Tommy questioned the victims.

'Was your box locked, Morrison?' he asked.

'I couldn't swear to it; but, dash it all, surely in a school like this it isn't necessary always to make sure of your things by locking your box? I thought somebody must have borrowed the ink-pot and forgotten to put it back. It's a beastly nuisance.'

'How about your box, Bellamy?'

'I locked it. I remember doing it. I always lock my box now in case some silly goat who wants to try and be funny should go and shove a beastly dead rat in it, all in among my fretwork.'

This had happened during the previous term, and it had

rankled in Bellamy's mind. He could still remember his feelings as his fingers, exploring the box in the dark, collided with the rat's limp corpse. He more than suspected Tommy of having placed the deceased there, but he had never been able to bring it home to him.

'All right, all right,' said Tommy, hastily. 'What a lot you do jaw, Bellamy! As if anybody would be likely to put a— However, we're wasting time. If your box was locked, how on earth did the chap, whoever he was, get at the chocolates? That's the rummy thing. I must think this over.'

By the end of the day it appeared that half the boys in the house had lost things. Clayton's air-pistol, with which he was wont in his spare time to shoot rubber-tipped darts against the walls of the dayroom (and occasionally against the backs of his friends' heads), had vanished, as Ram would have said, like snow before rays of sun. Ram himself had lost a curiously carved piece of wood, supposed (for no apparent reason) to be valuable. Others had lost various small objects. The worst loss was that of Sloper, who was in the habit of keeping a sort of reserve fund of silver in his box, wrapped up in a piece of paper. The paper was there, but the cash had gone. Fortunately, in a way, the reserve fund was at a low figure, owing to its owner's passion for Turkish delight, in which delicacy he had sunk most of his fortune; but still there was one-and-six, and in these hard times one-and-six is always one-and-six.

'It's jolly mysterious,' said Tommy. 'Because, you see, the rum thing is that most of the boxes from which things have gone were locked. Chaps remember locking them. Now, a fellow might have a key that happened to fit one box besides his own, or even two boxes, say. But when it comes to about a dozen, I don't see how the dickens he managed it. Besides, the chaps at this school aren't the sort of chaps who go about bagging things belonging to other people. I'm hanged if I know what to think about it.'

'Burglar,' suggested one of the Teeth.

'Silly ass,' said his brother, loftily.

'How do you mean, silly ass?'

'I mean silly ass, you silly ass. As if a burglar who broke into the house would be silly ass enough to bag penholders and things when he might be collaring plate.'

'Whose plate?'

'Spinder's plate, of course.'

'How do you know he's got any plate?'

'Of course he has. Everybody with a house has got plate.'

'Fat lot you know about it.'

'More than you, anyway.'

'Oh, chuck it,' said the company, wearily. This was too serious an occasion for Teeth rows. The twin brethren subsided, muttering, and the tea-bell, ringing shortly afterwards, put an end to the discussion.

When they reached their study, Tommy resumed the discussion with Jimmy. Jimmy's mind, full of his own anxieties, was not equal to taking much interest in petty thefts from play-boxes. He had lost a photograph frame from his own box, but he was not excited about it. The thought of the blue stone weighed on his mind. How was he to get it from Mr Spinder's possession? Where had the master hidden it? It must be somewhere in the study. Sam had thought so, for he had been searching it that night. It was the most likely place. But he could not think of any way of narrowing the search down. To be successful such a search must be long and careful. It was next to impossible to get into the study for the necessary length of time. Now that the master had been put on the alert by finding Sam and Marshall there, the risk of attempting a night visit was too great. It was a curious situation. Marshall, Ferris, and the lame man thought that he – Jimmy – still had the stone. Whereas, in reality, it was farther from his grasp than even from their own. They had methods of obtaining it, once they knew that Mr Spinder had it, which Jimmy lacked. School rules and regulations hampered Jimmy. The only times when it was certain that Mr Spinder would be out of his study – that is to say, during the hours of school work – Jimmy, by reason of this same school work, was unable to go into it. There seemed to be no solution to the problem.

Tommy, meanwhile, continued to discuss the mysterious play-box affair. To Tommy that was the important event of life at present. It took his mind for the time being even off the fascinating problem of what it was that Mr Spinder was keeping so carefully concealed behind the seventh book on his bookshelf.

He examined the matter from every point of view.

'It's the queerest thing I've ever known since I've been at the school,' he said. 'It's a regular Sherlock Holmes job. Isn't it curious about school; some terms nothing happens, and you feel as if you were going on forever just the same day after day, and then next term you are in the middle of all sorts of rows and excitements. I never dreamed this term was going to be half such fun. That fight between those two chaps in Spinder's study would have been enough by itself to make the term a success, and now this play-box business has come right on top of it.'

'I wonder what Spinder has done with that stone?' said Jimmy, meditatively.

'Great Scott! Are you still worrying about that rotten blue thing? I expect he's chucked it away by this time. I'll tell you something about Spinder that really is – no, I won't, though. Not yet, at any rate.'

Tommy wanted to keep his investigations into Mr Spinder's bookshelf a secret until they were complete. Half the fun of the thing would be gone if the secret was shared with anybody, even with Jimmy.

Jimmy said nothing. He had given up hope of trying to convince Tommy of the real value of the blue stone. Tommy still treated the whole matter as a very successful flight of imagination on the part of his friend. And Jimmy was content to leave it at that. Tommy, he thought, could be of no real assistance. He would be just as helpless in the circumstance as he was himself.

'I tell you what,' said Tommy, 'there's one thing I've thought of. Those things can't disappear from the play-boxes during the day. The thief, whoever he is, must go round at night after we're in bed. I tell you what. Tonight you and I will nip down into the dayroom and watch. Are you on?'

Jimmy only hesitated for a moment. Then his natural love of adventure asserted itself.

'All right,' he said.

On this occasion they had not the electric torch which they had used on their previous night ramble. They would not have used it in any case, as they wanted all the darkness they could get to conceal them; but they could not have had it, even if they had wished, for it was among the articles which had been stolen, greatly to its owner's grief.

It was pitch-dark in the room, and their shins suffered at first. Then they came to a standstill beside the further wall, where a cupboard, jutting out, would conceal them, provided the marauder did not carry with him too strong a light. And, for his own sake, he was not likely to do that.

Waiting in the dark was weary work, and several times Jimmy was minded to give it up and go back to bed; but Tommy's heart was so evidently in the business that he could not bring himself to leave him. They waited on for what seemed hours, till their ears, straining to catch the slightest sound, detected the soft pad-pad of stockinged feet. Tommy gripped Jimmy by the arm.

The unseen visitor was evidently one who knew his way about the room. He collided with nothing.

The footsteps ceased. There was a click. A sudden light shone out. They knew that light. It was the missing electric torch.

They could see a shadowy figure kneeling in front of a box, fumbling at the lock.

'Now!' whispered Tommy.

They darted forward, and flung themselves on him.

The struggle was short and sharp. Taken by surprise, the unknown looter of play-boxes made very little resistance after the first half-minute. His head had come into contact, as he fell, with the edge of a box, and this had discouraged him as much as anything.

The whole affair, except for the crack of the head on the box and the quick breathing of the three as they struggled, had been conducted with perfect quiet. The thief was just as anxious as were Jimmy and Tommy not to be heard.

Tommy sat on his man's chest and whispered to Jimmy to bring the torch, which lay some feet away. They turned the light on to the prisoner.

'Why, it's Wilkins!' said Jimmy.

Wilkins was the overgrown youth who cleaned the knives and boots of the house. Jimmy and Tommy had sometimes given him two-pence to fetch them biscuits and jam from the village after lock-up.

'Is that you, Mr Stewart?' whined the prostrate knife-and-boot expert. 'Let me up, Mr Stewart. I won't never do it again. Give a feller a chance, Mr Stewart.'

Tommy rapped him on the top of the head with his knuckles.

'Not so much of it,' he said severely. 'What were you playing at with these boxes? That's what we want to know? Buck up and tell us, or I'll jolly well screw your neck.'

'Oh, Mr Armstrong,' said Wilkins, 'do let me up. Don't be

'arsh on a feller, Mr Armstrong. I promise faithful it shan't 'appen again, Mr Armstrong. I—'

'Less of it – less of it,' said Tommy. 'Good heavens! The chap's a perfect gas-bag. You lie still for a bit and don't talk. I want to discuss this matter. If you jaw again till I tell you you may, I'll smother you.'

Wilkins subsided with a sniff.

'Now then, Jimmy,' said Tommy in a brisk undertone, 'what's to be done about this?'

'Oh, let him go,' said Jimmy. Now that the excitement was over he was tired of the whole thing, and wanted to get safely back to bed. Besides, though he knew that Wilkins deserved whatever he might get, he always felt sorry for anybody who was in a tight place. He did not wish to treat Wilkins with the severity which a stern moralist would have considered proper.

'Oh, thank yer, Mr Stewart, thank – ow!'

The last word was the result of a vigorous smack on the head from Tommy.

'Keep quiet, you worm!' said Tommy. 'Reserve your remarks till this court calls upon you to speak. By Jingo, if you interrupt again I'll give you a jab in the bazooka, which'll make you see stars for the rest of the night.'

Another sniff was the reply. Tommy turned to Jimmy again.

'Let him go?' he said. 'But, dash it, we've only just caught him.'

'I know. But it's no good getting the poor beast into the dickens of a row. If you let him go now he'll probably turn over a what-d'you-call-it – new leaf, I mean. Let's make him give back the things he's bagged, and then let him go.'

Tommy reflected.

'All right,' he said at last. 'I suppose we may as well. It'll be a lesson to him. And, by Jove, I forgot! There's another reason. Tell you later.'

It had suddenly dawned upon Tommy that his own and Jimmy's position in this matter was more than a little questionable. True, they had caught the thief. But they had broken out of their dormitory and climbed the locked railing at the end of the passage to do it; and there was no doubt that, after the authorities had made it warm for Wilkins for stealing, they would proceed to make it more than a little warm for the captors for breaking school rules. This had the effect of quenching

Tommy's zeal for arresting malefactors. In the detective stories the detective does not have to think whether he will get caned or given lines after he has captured his man. He can concentrate his mind on the capture. This, thought Tommy, gives him an unfair advantage over the amateur detective at school.

'All right,' he said, 'we'll let you go. But you've jolly well got to put back everything you've bagged. You can leave them somewhere in here where the chaps will find them.'

'Oh, thank yer, thank yer, Mr Armstrong and Mr Stewart; but I've ate the chocolates.'

'Well, you needn't worry about those, then. I only hope they made you ill. But all the rest of the things – see?'

'Yes, Mr Armstrong.'

'Tomorrow morning, first thing.'

'Yes, Mr Armstrong.'

'And now,' said Tommy, 'before I let you up, you can go ahead and tell us how you managed to open these boxes. That's what's been puzzling me.'

'I was led away, Mr Armstrong.'

'Don't be an ass. That doesn't account for it. You can't open a locked play-box simply by being led away.'

'It was the chap wot led me away wot give me the key.'

'What key?'

'He called it a skellington key.'

'Skeleton key! Ah, that accounts for it. Now we *are* getting hold of something, as the bulldog said when he bit the tramp's Sunday trousers.'

Wilkins laughed respectfully, but was discouraged with a rap on the head.

'Don't giggle there like a hyæna,' said Tommy sternly. 'What you've got to do is to fix your mind on the painful details, and tell me them in a low, clear voice. Who's this chap you're talking about – the chap who gave you the key? And what on earth did he give you the key for?'

'He wanted me to find him something in Mr Stewart's box—'

'What!' cried Jimmy, suddenly interested.

'Yes, Mr Stewart. He said it was a small blue stone, what looked like a piece of sealing-wax, and I was to take it from your box and he'd give me half a crown for it. And he give me the key. He said it would open any box – it didn't matter what sort of lock it was; and, being easily led away, I tried some of the boxes, and—'

'By Jove, Jimmy, then you were right after all!' said Tommy excitedly. 'That rummy stone was really worth something. I thought you were only piling it on about it for a lark. By Jove, this is getting interesting! Go on, you blighter. Who was the man?'

'I 'adn't never set eyes on him before, Mr Armstrong.'

'Was it a biggish, clean-shaven man, with queer-looking eyes?' asked Jimmy. It was the nearest he could get to a description of Marshall.

'No, Mr Stewart. He was a stout man with a moustache. He talked rather slow and pleasant-like. Sort of like a cat, he reminded me.'

'Ferris!' cried Jimmy. So this was a sample of Ferris's methods! He could not help admitting that they were subtler than Marshall's, as Ferris himself had said. But for the accident of the stone having passed in the first instance out of Jimmy's possession it would have been in the play-box, and the move would have been successful. Jimmy felt that Ferris was more to be feared than Marshall. Ferris could strike where Marshall could not. Wilkins' comparison of him to a cat struck him as particularly apt. It was that smooth, cat-like quality in him which made him so formidable as a foe.

'Have you got the key?' asked Tommy. 'Oh, it's in that lock now, is it? Well, I'll keep it, I think. It's a useful thing to have about the house. Now,' he said, rising, 'you can clear out. We needn't detain you.'

Wilkins began to utter profuse expressions of gratitude, but was cut short. He slid noiselessly from the room; and Tommy and Jimmy, bearing the electric torch to light their way, returned hurriedly to their dormitory.

'I say, Jimmy,' said Tommy, sitting on his bed, 'this has been a bit of an eye-opener. I'd no notion you weren't simply rotting about that blue stone of yours. Do you mean to say these fellows really are after it?'

Jimmy related briefly the events which had taken place in the cottage. Tommy's eyes bulged as he listened.

'My word!' he gasped.

There was a silence while he rearranged his view on the whole matter, and examined it afresh in the light of this new information.

'Do you mean to say they *shot* at you?' he said at last.

Jimmy nodded.

'I say!' said Tommy.

'But, dash it, you ought to do something,' he went on. 'I mean it's *dangerous*.'

'It is a bit,' agreed Jimmy with a short laugh. 'But what can I do?'

'Why, tell the— No, you can't do that. Not tell the police, I mean. They wouldn't believe you any more than I did.'

'No.'

'The queer part about it is that these fellows are after the wrong man the whole time. They really don't want you at all, if they only knew it. They want Spinder; he's got the stone.'

'I know he has – somewhere. I wish I knew where.'

Tommy leaped excitedly from his bed.

'I know where it is! Great Scott, of course. Do you remember, when we were hiding in his study, seeing him—'

'I couldn't see him from where I was.'

'Nor you could. Well, I saw him go to one of the shelves, pull out a book, and take out something from behind it. It was the stone, of course. I can see that now. Well, when he was ragging me in his room yesterday, the Head sent for him, and I was left alone. So I nipped to the shelf and began lugging out the books. I'd just pulled out the seventh, and felt there was something small and hard behind it, when he came back, and I had only just time to shove the book in again.'

It was Jimmy's turn to be excited.

'Are you sure?' he said eagerly.

'Absolutely certain.'

Jimmy sprang to his feet.

'Let's go down now and look,' he said.

They left the room and made the difficult journey a second time, creeping stealthily down the stairs and along the corridor to the master's study.

They stopped at the door. There was no light underneath it. Jimmy seized the handle, turned it gently, and pushed. The door did not open. He pushed again, but with no result.

'Locked,' he whispered.

'He must have started locking it after that fight between Sam and the man,' said Tommy. 'We'd better get back.'

'Yes; we must look out for another chance.' They crept upstairs again to their dormitory.

The next day was the day of the football match. Most of the members of the team spent their spare time during the morning practising shooting goals with crumpled-up balls of paper, and Bellamy, who was to keep goal, being a youth who believed in taking no chances, was observed sitting in a corner studying 'Hints to Young Goal-keepers,' by a Scottish international. He thought it might contain one or two tips which would come in useful in the heat of the struggle.

As Jimmy was standing in the road by the school that morning, a village boy addressed him.

'Could you tell Ji—'

He held out a note.

'Let's have a look,' said Jimmy. He glanced at the note. It was addressed to himself, written in pencil in a hand that was strange to him. 'That's all right,' he said. 'It's for me. Thanks.'

He opened it. It was from Sam Burrows.

'Mr Stewart,' it ran. 'Sir – Must see you if possible today. Very important. Hear you are playing football at the College today. Should respectfully request you meet me at the first milestone as you leave College at five sharp. Please be there, as matter is very important. – SAML. BURROWS.'

Jimmy stared at the note thoughtfully. He reread it. What could this thing be about which Sam wished to see him? He wished he had given a hint in the note, but recollected that it might not have been safe. The note was written on a scrap of paper, not enclosed in an envelope.

He had not seen Sam since that day when he had told him of the loss of the stone, and he had wondered at the latter's silence. Where had he been all this time? Why had he sent no message? However, he would soon know. He resolved to bicycle to the match, instead of riding with the others in the brake. That would give him an opportunity of slipping away. He could ride on and catch them up after he had seen Sam. Or he could slip away before the brake started. Bowdon would probably ask him to tea. He could go to tea and come away early. The team would know where he had gone, and would not expect to see him again till they returned to the school.

He showed the note to Tommy. Tommy, greatly interested, suggested that he should come too; but Jimmy thought not. Sam would prefer to see him alone.

'I tell you what,' said Tommy. 'I've been thinking this business over, and I see the force of what you told me that fellow Marshall said in the cottage about the difficulty of getting at a chap at school. I think you're all right as long as you stick to the rest of us. You're sure there's no risk of them getting you if you come home alone?'

'Oh, no. They wouldn't tackle me while Sam was there. Sam's got a revolver.'

'How about the air-gun?'

'They won't get him that way again. There's no cover by that milestone. They couldn't hide near enough to shoot. Besides, it's pretty dark about five o'clock. They couldn't see to aim from a distance. I shall be all right.'

'I hope so,' said Tommy doubtfully. 'I wish you'd let me come.'

* * *

The match was due to begin at half-past two. It was a dry, cold day, with a rather strong wind blowing across the ground. The Marleigh team took the field, somewhat nervous. They were playing away from home – which is always a handicap to a football team – and the jaunty confidence of the College boys tended to make them think less of themselves. The only unconcerned member of the eleven was Bellamy, who perused his 'Hints to Young Goal-keepers' till the last possible moment, putting the book away in his great-coat pocket with reluctance when the teams began to strip.

'I'd only got to page eighty-one,' he confided to Jimmy in an aggrieved tone. 'Still, I've got hold of some useful information. I think we shall be all right.'

He was the only one of the eleven who did think so. The rest were unmistakably nervous. Even Jimmy felt doubtful, and Tommy was remarkably subdued.

The Alderton team filed on to the ground, looking very trim and workmanlike. Bowdon came across and shook hands with Jimmy.

'Hullo!' he said. 'Feeling fit?'

'Pretty well, thanks. Where are you playing?'

'Outside right. Where are you?'

'Right back.'

'Oh, then we shan't meet, I suppose. By the way, you ought to see O'Connell. He's a different man. You seem to have knocked all the side out of him. It was a splendid thing for him. Come in and have some tea in my study afterwards?'

'Thanks awfully.'

'Good. Oh, I say, how's your pal – the black man who recited? All right?'

'Splendid. Hullo, they're just going to start.'

'So they are. Well, see you afterwards.'

'Right ho. Thanks.'

Bowdon trotted to his place, and the referee blew his whistle.

It was evident from the first that the College team thought little of the capabilities of their opponents. They started with a cheerful confidence in their own powers, which had the effect of upsetting the Marleigh eleven still further. A little tricky passing, and the ball was in the visitors' territory. Bowdon, racing down on the right, tricked Tommy, made for the corner flag, and centred. The Alderton centre forward steadied himself for a moment, then banged the ball hard and tight into the corner of the net. Alderton was one up after two minutes' play.

Bellamy, the goal-keeper, had stood stock still while the shot was being made.

'For goodness' sake get to them, Bellamy,' said Jimmy. 'You didn't move.'

'I know,' said Bellamy indignantly. 'It was all that book. It's a beastly fraud. That was one of the cases mentioned in the second chapter. By right that man ought to have shot along dotted line A to B, clean into my hands. Instead of which he let me down by sending the ball into the corner. I'm going to forget that book for the rest of the game.'

'I should,' said Jimmy. 'We don't want to get licked by double figures.'

That early goal had two effects. It increased the self-confidence of the Alderton team to just beyond that point where self-confidence is a good thing; and it stung the Marleigh eleven into activity. The feeling of strangeness and nervousness wore off, leaving only a determination to play their own game and win if they could.

A stout attack by the forwards was stopped by the Alderton backs, and the ball returned to the Marleigh half. The College forwards began to attack again. But their over-confidence robbed the movement of all its force. Instead of going hard for the goal they wasted time in exhibition passing and trick-work. It baffled the Marleigh halves, but Tommy and Jimmy, lying behind them, found no difficulty in tackling. The fact was that the College team was suffering the curious effect of being too scientific. Every year in the cup ties one sees instances of what is plainly the less skilful team beating by rugged, straightforward play a team that plays too clever a game.

This was what happened now. The College forwards did surprising things with the ball. They passed with the greatest neatness, and tricked their men time after time. They did everything, in fact, but score goals. Whereas Marleigh, when they attacked, did it with a direct purpose which was infinitely more effective.

After twenty minutes' play, Morrison, running straight through in the centre, slung the ball across to Jarvis on the left. Jarvis sprinted straight down the touchline, dodged the back, and centred. Morrison got to the ball just before the goal-keeper, and headed it through. The scores were now equal.

This unexpected reverse sobered the College team. Their forwards abandoned their exhibition tactics, and endeavoured to get through. But Marleigh was now on its mettle. Tommy and Jimmy at back were not to be passed. Time after time they cleared with long kicks which gave their forward line chances of which they availed themselves. The scientific College forwards were knocked off the ball again and again till their combination became ragged and uncertain. The College goal-keeper was kept busy.

Just before half-time, stopping a hot shot from Morrison, he could not get rid of the ball at once, and Binns, who had come up from centre half to join in the attack, rushed in and hustled him over the line.

Marleigh crossed over at half-time a goal to the good.

Alderton never recovered the lost ground. Bowdon made some good runs on his wing, but the team, as a team, were all to pieces. They passed wildly. They lost their heads, and dribbled when they should have passed. The wind, which was now blowing straight down the ground, helped Tommy and Jimmy with their clearing kicks; and when, shortly after the restart, Sloper scored with a long dropping shot, the thing became a rout. Marleigh had all the game. Bellamy was only called upon to save twice more, on which occasions, relying on his own methods, he kept the ball out with great success. Ten minutes later Morrison shot the fourth goal. And when the whistle blew the score was six to one in favour of Marleigh. The College team left the field with rather less jauntiness than they had entered it. Marleigh strolled off with a careless air, as if that sort of thing was a mere nothing to them.

Tommy went home with the others in the brake, leaving Jimmy with Bowdon. He was not easy in his mind. He was vaguely afraid. Jimmy should have taken him to the rendezvous in case of accidents.

He went to his study and waited. He waited for what seemed to him quite a long time. Surely, he thought, Jimmy should have been back by now. He looked at his watch. A quarter-past six. It was queer.

Half-past six came and went, and a quarter to seven. Tommy began to feel more than vaguely uneasy. He was almost certain now that something must have happened.

Five to seven.

He went into the road, and looked out along it.

There were no signs of Jimmy. It was empty.

Tommy stood and looked down the road for fully ten minutes before he saw anyone on it; and when somebody did appear, it was not Jimmy, but a man, a sturdy, thickly built man, whom the most careless observer could have told as an old soldier from the set of his shoulders and the swing of his walk.

He was shabbily dressed, and Tommy took him at first for a tramp. He watched him approach, and wondered mildly if he would try to get anything from him. When the man, coming nearer, saw him, and hurried on towards him, Tommy had made up his mind that he and two-pence must part company. He was feeling in his pocket as the man halted before him.

'Beg pardon, sir.'

Tommy began to draw his hand, with the two-pence in it, out of his pocket.

'Do you belong to the school, sir?'

'Yes. Why?' said Tommy.

'Do you 'appen to know a young gentleman of the name of Stewart?'

Tommy jumped.

'What!' he cried. 'Stewart?'

'Master Jimmy Stewart.'

'Great Scott, yes. Why—'

'Chum of yours, maybe?'

'Yes, I should rather say so. We share a study. But what—'

The man lowered his voice.

'It's like this, matey,' he said. 'I want to see 'im particular, and there's reasons why it wouldn't quite do for me to walk up to the front door and say, "Is Master Stewart at 'ome?" I want to see him private about something as concerns only 'im and me. You couldn't take me a message to him, could you, matey?'

'He isn't in.'

'Not in? Where's he to, then?'

'There was a footer match on this afternoon at Alderton College. Jimmy was playing, and has stopped to tea with one of the chaps.'

Tommy had decided to use this version of the case, if questioned.

'Ah,' said the man. 'Well, when he comes back I'd take it kind if you'd tell him Corporal Sam Burrows called to—'

'Sam Burrows!' gasped Tommy. A chill sensation of impending disaster came over him. If this was Sam Burrows, why had he not met Jimmy? And where was Jimmy?

'That's me, matey. Know the name?'

'But,' cried Tommy, 'what are you doing here? What's happened to Jimmy? Why didn't you meet him?'

The soldier flashed a puzzled look at him from under his thick eyebrows.

'What's all this, matey?' he said sharply. 'All this about meeting the Colonel's nipper. What are you driving at?'

'The letter you wrote!' stammered Tommy.

The other's face became very grave.

'How's that? A letter? I wrote no letter.'

Tommy stared at him with a growing fear at his heart.

'You didn't write that letter?' he muttered.

The soldier shook him roughly by the shoulder with a strong, brown hand.

'Pull yourself together, mate,' he said quickly. 'Tell me what you mean. This looks bad. Tell me what it is you're driving at.'

'The letter!' said Tommy. 'Jimmy got a letter this morning signed with your name, telling him to meet you at the first milestone from the college gates at five o'clock today. That's where he's gone.'

Sam Burrows swore a full-bodied oath.

'The devils!' he cried. 'They've got him. My lord, they've got him. See here, which is the way to this college you're talking about?'

Tommy pointed down the road.

'It's straight along the road you came down. Look here,' he added, 'I'll come with you. I shall get into a row, but that doesn't matter. I know all about this business. Jimmy told me. I thought he was ragging at first, but after what he told me last night—'

'What was that?'

Tommy related the story of what had happened in the cottage, as told him by Jimmy, Sam swearing softly at intervals by way of accompaniment.

'Ferris,' he said, when Tommy had finished. 'Never 'eard of 'im. So they've got a new man in to help, have they? Well, I hope I'll lay my hands on him one of these days. I'll stop his games. See here, matey, we must hurry. Lord knows what's happened out there.'

'They wouldn't kill him, would they?' faltered Tommy.

'All depends. They'd stick at nothing, they wouldn't. Kill a man as soon as look at 'im if it suited their book. Come on, sonny. We must run.'

They started off down the road at a jog-trot. Tommy, tired with his efforts in the football match, soon found this too much for him. He stopped.

'You go on,' he panted. 'I can't keep up. I'll follow.'

But at this moment a cart turned into the main road from a lane just behind them. Sam hailed it.

'Going down the road, matey?'

'Ay.'

'Couldn't give us a lift, could you?'

'Jump up.'

'That's a bit of luck,' said Sam to Tommy, as they scrambled in. 'Get there in no time now.'

The cart bowled on till they could see the top portions of the college buildings over the brow of the hill.

'Best get off here,' said Sam.

They thanked the driver, and dropped off. The cart rumbled on.

It was quite dark now, a fact which caused Sam to look gloomy.

'Don't give a man no chance,' he said, 'this bloomin' darkness. I can do a bit of tracking by daylight, but blow me if I can manage it now. We shall have to trust to luck.'

'Shall we shout?' said Tommy.

'It won't do no 'arm.'

Tommy let out a yell of the sort with which he was accustomed to crack the plaster on the ceiling of the dayroom at the school. They waited.

'No good,' said Sam. 'We'll—'

'Listen!' said Tommy, clutching him by the arm.

They stopped, and strained their ears.

'I don't hear nothing,' said Sam.

'I'll try again.' He uttered another shout. 'Now!'

This time there was certainly an answer, very faint and seeming to come from far away.

'He's in the fields somewhere,' said Sam. 'If it's him. It sounded a precious long way away.'

'Come on,' said Tommy.

They left the road, and plunged into the fields at the side. Every now and then Tommy stopped to shout, and gradually the answering cries grew more distinct.

Presently, on the left, a building could be seen dimly in the darkness. Tommy shouted once more, and this time the answer came from quite close at hand. Followed closely by Sam, Tommy made a dash for the building.

'He's in there,' he cried. 'Jimmy!'

The building, they could see now, was a ruined cottage of the usual one-storey type. The door was open. They rushed in.

'Who's that?' said a faint voice. 'Is that you, Tommy? Here I am. Against this wall.'

Tommy felt his way along the walls till his hand touched a shoulder.

'I'm tied up,' said Jimmy. 'Get a knife.'

Sam struck a match. The light, burning up, fell on Jimmy's face. He looked tired and worn.

Tommy was hacking with his knife at the cords. It was difficult work, for they were thick and the knife blunt; but he managed it at last. Jimmy staggered to his feet, then fell in a heap with a cry of pain.

'Cramp,' said Sam briefly, dropping the match and beginning to rub Jimmy's legs. After a while Jimmy got to his feet again. He could stand now, but he was evidently weak. Sam lit another match, and produced a flask. Jimmy drank from it, and the effects were immediate.

'It's all right,' he said, 'I'm better now. Thanks, Sam.'

'Look here, Jimmy,' cried Tommy, 'can you walk? How are you feeling? Don't try to talk about it yet. Wait a bit.'

'My bike's somewhere about,' said Jimmy. 'They brought it in here. There it is.'

'How are we to get out into the road again? I don't know how we got here.'

'It's quite simple. There's only one field to cross. This is the same cottage they found me in before.'

'Let's make a move,' said Tommy. 'Jimmy, that letter wasn't from Sam at all. It was a trick. Come on, though. Don't talk.'

They reached the road.

'I'm all right now,' said Jimmy. 'I'll tell you what happened. By Jove, I'm glad you came. I thought I should never get out of that beastly place. I had almost given up hope. Let's sit down here for a bit. I want to rest, if I'm going to get back to the school.'

'If they come back,' said Sam grimly, 'I'll be ready for them.' He pulled something out of his pocket, and kept it in his hand while he listened. 'Well, matey, what happened?'

'I got away from Bowdon's study at about ten to five, and biked to the milestone. It was just five by my watch when I reached it. I couldn't see Sam anywhere about, so I propped my bike up against the hedge, and sat down on the milestone to wait for him. I was a bit fagged after the game, and I must have gone half to sleep, for I suddenly woke up with a start, feeling there was someone just behind me. You know. That queer feeling you get in a darkish room sometimes. I was just going to turn round, when a hand slid over my mouth, and somebody jerked me back and knelt on my chest. I was too surprised to resist. I just lay there, and they tied me up and carried me across the field to the cottage, Marshall and Ferris. It was the first time I've seen Ferris close to. He's a fat chap. An awful brute.' Jimmy shuddered.

'Well?' said Tommy eagerly.

'They got me in there, and then they started to search me. I think they were a bit rattled at not finding the stone on me. At any rate, Ferris was. You see, he knew it was not in my play-box, so he thought I must carry it about on me. Well, when they couldn't find it, they began cursing and threatening me. I swore I hadn't got the stone. I said I'd lost it soon after I got back to school after the holidays. They wouldn't believe me, and Ferris – he's the worst of the lot, an awful brute – got hold of me and tied me up to a beam, so that only my toes were on the ground. It was a frightful strain on my wrists. I nearly yelled – it hurt so. Ferris said he'd keep me like that till I told them where the stone was. I kept on saying I hadn't got it. They wouldn't believe me, and at last the strain got so bad I suppose I must have fainted. At any rate, I heard them jawing to one another in a rum sort of language I didn't understand, and then the words began to run into one another, and everything got all dark, and the next thing I remember was finding myself on the floor, propped up against the wall, still tied up and feeling awfully sick. Then, after what seemed hours, I heard you shouting.'

Sam looked thoughtful.

'You didn't say as how it was Mr Spinder what had really got the blue ruin, did you, Master Stewart?'

'No. I simply said I hadn't got it.'

Sam nodded.

'They'll guess,' he said. 'Trust them. That Marshall, as you call him, knows it was me he found burglaring Mr Spinder's study, and he knows only one thing what would take me out a-committing of burglary. Yes, they'll be on the track precious soon. It's your Mr Spinder what's got the hornets' nest on to him now. You and me, Master Jimmy, we're put on one side. It's a what you might call a triangular tournament like what didn't 'appen between England, Australia, and South Africa at cricket. It's a all-against-all game, this is. And it'll be us as'll win, or I'll know the reason why. I'll pay them, the whole bloomin' crew of 'em, if I can get to arm's length of 'em. And now we're all a-gettin' ready for the bloomin' last match of the tournament, what'll be played on Mr Spinder's ground. And I don't envy him, neither. Are you ready, Master Jimmy? We'd best be moving on.'

Tommy chuckled.

'It's rather rummy, when you come to think of it,' he said, 'that tonight's business will simply end in your getting a hundred lines from Spinder for being late for lock-up.'

Morning school at Marleigh was over by half-past twelve, and afternoon school did not begin till two o'clock. Mr Spinder had just entered his study at half-past one on the following day, when the servant appeared to say that a gentleman wished to see him.

'Gentleman? What name?' asked Mr Spinder.

'He wouldn't give no name, sir.'

'Well, show him in,' said Mr Spinder. He spoke irritably, for he had been looking forward to a rest before afternoon school began.

The servant left the room, returning shortly with the visitor. He was a sleek, stout man, with a curious, fixed half-smile always on his face. He looked almost like a man wearing some sort of mask. Only a very poor student of character would have set him down as the amiable, easy-going person he looked at a first glance.

'Good afternoon,' said Mr Spinder. 'Will you take a seat?'

'Thanks. I hope to take more than a seat before I go,' was the reply, in a smooth voice which matched the smooth face. 'I believe I am addressing Mr Spinder?'

'You are,' said Mr Spinder shortly. 'Well?'

The servant had left the room and shut the door. The visitor moved softly to it, and flung it open. He looked up and down the passage, then returned to his seat.

'Servants,' he said blandly, 'are worthy creatures, but they sometimes stay much too near keyholes. Yours, however, does not seem to suffer from the sad vice of inquisitiveness.'

Mr Spinder tapped the floor with his foot.

'I should be glad if you would kindly—'

'Just so, just so. I can put the thing in a nutshell. It is much better to be brief. I want that little blue stone, Mr Spinder.'

Mr Spinder tried to restrain a start, but he could not wholly succeed. The other noted it with a slight broadening of his placid smile.

'What do you mean?' said the master. 'What is this nonsense about blue stones? I must remind you that I am a busy man, and that if this is a joke—'

The visitor waved his hand deprecatingly.

'Just so, just so,' he said. 'But couldn't we skip all that, Mr Spinder? It would save such a lot of time, and, as you say, you are a busy man. So am I. So don't let us waste time. You know you have that stone. I know you have. You know I know you have. So why not let us be open and frank about it, and talk it over quietly and comfortably?'

Mr Spinder made a sudden dash for one of the drawers in the writing-table, and pulled out a revolver.

'This is loaded,' he said shortly, pointing it at his visitor.

The latter's smile almost became a grin. He raised his eyebrows.

'My dear sir,' he said, 'really! How very crude you are! Quite like poor dear old Marshall. Do you really think that I should attempt violence, when I have been admitted at your front door and am in the middle of a crowd of servants and boys and I don't know what? I can assure you I have far more respect for my neck than to risk it like that. I am here in the perfectly peaceful capacity of ambassador. I am anxious to know on what terms you would part with the stone? We are prepared to pay anything reasonable, for, to be frank with you, time is a consideration, and, while we shall undoubtedly get the stone in the end, whether you sell it or not, the process might be rather a long one.'

'That,' said Mr Spinder, 'is quite true.'

'But why consider such a possibility?' went on the visitor. 'You are a sensible man, and will not cause us this inconvenience, I am sure. To come to bedrock, Mr Spinder, how much?'

'I am sorry, but it is not for sale.'

'No, no, no, Mr Spinder, really. Think again.'

'It is not for sale.'

'A thousand pounds. You could do a great deal with a thousand pounds, a man with your intellect.'

'It is not for sale.'

'Five thousand pounds. You could do even more with five thousand pounds, could you not?'

'You have had my answer.'

'Not your final answer, I hope. Shall we say ten thousand pounds?'

Mr Spinder rose and moved to the bell.

'I need not detain you,' he said.

'One moment, one moment. No need to ring in any case. I can find my way out. Would twenty thousand pounds be more to your taste? Think of it, Mr Spinder! Twenty thousand pounds! A fortune!'

Mr Spinder took up a book, and began to turn the leaves.

'You will forgive me if I read,' he said. 'This conversation is beginning to tire me. Pray continue, however, if it amuses you.'

The visitor's eyes gleamed viciously, but his voice was as smooth as ever when he spoke.

'I am sorry to interrupt your reading,' he said. 'You are holding the book upside down, by the way. May I ask, apologising if the question is impertinent, why you persist in this refusal? You do not propose to give the stone to Colonel Stewart?'

'Colonel Stewart? I have never heard of him.'

'Then why refuse twenty thousand pounds?'

Mr Spinder shut his book with a bang.

'Suppose you had a gold mine, Mr—'

'Never mind my name. You were saying—'

'Suppose you had a gold mine, would you part with it to a man who offered you sixpence for it?'

'I fail to see the connection very clearly, Mr Spinder. You mean—'

'You are offering me sixpence for my gold mine. Do you suppose I intend to let you have this stone for a mere twenty thousand pounds? I might just as well give it to you.'

'You don't think twenty thousand pounds a very large sum, then? Well, well, opinions differ. I should be glad enough of it. Would thirty thousand suit you better?'

'Not in the least.'

'You are a man of large ideas, Mr Spinder!'

'Exactly. I happen to be one of the few men in England who know what this stone is, and what is its real worth. I intend to see that I am paid full value for it. I don't know whom you are representing, though I suspect. At least, I know that there are people who want this stone very much indeed, and can afford to pay more than thirty thousand pounds for it.'

'Then—'

'When your employers, whoever they are, offer me two hundred and fifty thousand pounds, I may begin to consider it.'

'You certainly are a man of large ideas. Have you reflected, though, that you will find it a little difficult to dispose of this stone? We are the only buyers in the market. The other party would merely take the stone, if you approached them with it, and probably put you in prison for a lengthy period for having it in your possession? Have you considered that?'

'I have. You say you are the only buyers in the market. Quite so. But, you see, you cannot afford not to buy, whereas I can afford to wait. Perhaps you will tell your employers that, and add that delay in buying may very possibly mean that my price will go up. I think that now we may end this little discussion, may we not?'

The visitor rose, his suave manner laid aside.

'You fool,' he hissed. 'You sit there talking simply of buying and selling. Have you thought that there is another way? We are not men whom it is well to thwart, Mr Spinder. You are treading a dangerous path. You will be watched every hour of the day. Sooner or later you must fall into our hands. And then – well, I think you will wish you had accepted my offer.'

'I will risk it,' said Mr Spinder curtly. 'Good afternoon.'

The visitor recovered himself. He picked up his hat.

'Good afternoon, Mr Spinder. I may take it, then, that our offer is definitely refused?'

'You may.'

'Quite so, quite so. We shall have to think of another way. I am sorry for you, Mr Spinder.'

Mr Spinder motioned towards the door. With a nod and a smile the visitor passed out.

Scarcely had he gone, when Mr Spinder, locking the door, darted to the bookshelf, and took out the seventh book. He thrust his hand into the cavity. Then he uttered a cry like that of an animal. With wild haste he tore book after book from their places, and hurled them on to the floor. The whole shelf was bare now. He ran his hand from end to end of it, but his fingers found nothing.

The blue stone was gone.

About two hours before Mr Spinder made the discovery which caused so great an upheaval of his mind, Herr Steingruber, stolidly patient as ever, had been endeavouring to drive into the heads of his class the mysteries of his native language. It was a thankless job, and one which a lesser man would have thrown up long before. But the Herr, in whose character dogged patience was a leading trait, had never lost heart. Not even the massive stupidity of Bellamy could discourage him.

Bellamy was translating at the present moment, in a slow, dreamy style, admirably designed to show up his mistakes. The German master plucked in a distracted way at his hair as the stout one ambled on.

'Ach, no, no!' he moaned.

Bellamy looked up, surprised, almost pained. He made another shot. The German master's agony increased.

'Wrong; horrible id is,' he cried.

Bellamy, after staring goggle-eyed at him for a moment, apparently gave the thing up as a bad job. He produced a nib from his pocket, stuck it into the desk, and began flipping it meditatively with his forefinger. The musical twang roused the German master like a trumpet-blast.

'What vos dat?' he cried.

'That, sir? What, sir?' answered half a dozen eager voices.

So far the lesson had been on the dull side, and the interruption was welcome.

'Dat zound. Dat like zome musigal instdrumend far away blaying zound. Vas it in der room?'

'I don't think so, sir,' said Binns. 'I rather fancy it's a harpsichord, sir, playing out in the road. I'll go and stop it, sir, shall I?'

'Do your seat, Pinns! Do your seat dis momend redurn,' cried Herr Steingruber wildly, as Binns began to move swiftly to the door.

'All right, sir,' said Binns agreeably. 'I only wanted to help.'

'Dat vos kindt of you, Pinns,' said the Herr, mollified, 'but not a harbzichord do I dthink dot it vos, but zomething in dis room.'

'Perhaps a mouse, sir,' suggested Sloper.

'Berhaps a mouze. Jah, but berhaps nod, I dthink. No, it vos like zome zo strange und faint musigal instdrumend, var, var away blaying. Ach, vell, dis vos nod der deaching of der Sherman language, zo? Dis vos der idle chadder und dimewasding. Zo, Pellamy, vill you gontinue?'

Bellamy, who had broken the nib in extracting from it a fortissimo note, was at liberty to return to the lesson. He went on at the place where he had left off, but his performance did not improve. After a couple of lines Herr Steingruber stopped him, and informed the class that he would relate a little story with a moral. The Herr's stories were always extremely long, and consequently formed an admirable break in the actual work of the class. For that reason, if for no other, they were eagerly welcomed. The class settled itself comfortably to hear what he had to say.

'In der zity of London,' began the Herr impressively, 'I vas do my pank der odder day broceeding do gash a liddle cheg—'

'How much for, sir?' inquired Morrison, who was a stickler

for detail, especially when it made for a longer postponement of work.

'It does nod madder, der amound of der cheg.'

'Still, it makes it so much more interesting, knowing, sir,' argued Morrison.

'Yes, sir,' said Sloper. 'It makes the whole thing so much more real.'

'Ach, zo! Bot der exagged amoundt I gannot ad dis momend glearly regollegt. Bot I dthink dot it was doo bounds vour shil-langs. Berhabs a liddle more.'

'Let's call it two pound ten, shall we, sir?' said Binns.

'No, no, it vos nod krite zo moch as dat. Nod nearly krite zo moch.'

'Two pound five, then, sir,' suggested Sloper.

'And six,' said Morrison.

'Zo, zo, zo. Doo bound vive and zix. Bot, I dell you, id does nod madder, id does nod madder. Of der liddle cheg der amound vos immaderial. Zo. I vos going droo der zity of London—'

'What street, sir?' asked Morrison.

'I do nod der sdreed regollegt.'

'Was it Threadneedle Street, sir? My father has an office there.'

'Was it near the Mansion House?'

'Or St Paul's, sir? I once went to a service at St Paul's.'

The Herr waved his arms protestingly.

'Dot vos all immaderial, all immaderial. Id does nod madder, nod der amound of der cheg nor der name of der sdreed. Vhot I am delling you is dis. I vos droo der sdreed – let us zay, if you on a name inzist, Lompard Sdreed—'

Morrison thought for a moment of asking which side of Lombard Street, but decided not to push the point. Sloper, how-ever, was less restrained.

'Anywhere near the England and Europe Bank, sir? My father banks there. I went there once with him.'

'Zo,' said the Herr patiently, 'let us zay id vos near der Enkland and Eurobe Bangk, then. Id vos all immaderial. Vell, I vos along der bavemend broceeding, dthinging of dthings within myself, vhen a man in der road, in der cutter, you understandt, he say do me, "Puy a doy, sir? Puy a doy?" He vos, you understandt, a – as you would zay – a hawker, a beddler, und he had a dray pefore him of liddle doys full.'

'What sort of toys, sir?' inquired Morrison.

'All der ladest doys. Der wriggling znake, und der wrestling men, und der exbiring roosder, und gollar-sduds.'

'You can't call a collar-stud a toy,' objected Binns.

'He is under der heading of doys in dis gase gombrised, because der man vos zelling him wit der odder doys, all on von dray.

'Vell, I do der man turned, und I zay, "No, dthangk you, my goot man; I have nod of a doy any need." Ad der zame time, as I looged ad him, dere zeemed zomething aboud his face dot of zomebody I had once med zomehow zeemed to remind me. Bot I vos dthinging no more aboud id, yen he say to me, "Von't you puy a gollar-stud for der zake of old times?"'

'Why a collar-stud?' objected Morrison. 'Why not a toy?'

Herr Steingruber waved the interruption aside. He saw the point of his story well in sight, and he was making for it with the earnest concentration of a horse which knows that it is heading for its stables.

'I looged ad der man glosely, und I say, "For old dimes, my goot man! Vhot vos dot you mean by zaying a zo gurious dthing?" Und he durn his vace up do mine, und he say, "Ach, my old poyhood vriend und gollege gombanion Hans, is id dot I am zo by misvortune und brivations changed dot you do not regognise me?" Und den I bog more garefully sdill, und I zee dot id is my old vriend Fritz Müller dot I have nod for many years, nod since we were vellow-sdudents und inzebarable goot vriends at der university of Heidelberg, met. Und I zay to him, shogged und sdardled' – here the Herr, to add point to the narrative, assumed a look of intense agitation and threw his arms above his head – 'I zay to him, "Fritz, vhat is id dot you do dis zo great distress und misfortune has brought?" Und he shed a zad dear.'

This was too much for the class. Their feelings were outraged. Every nerve in their bodies resented Fritz's degraded conduct.

'What, sir!' they cried. 'Did he blub?'

Herr Steingruber gazed round impressively, mistaking the disgust of the class at Fritz's disgraceful exhibition for horror at the reduced condition of that unfortunate.

'Zo,' he said. 'Jah! He shed der zad dear, und he zay, "Vhat vos it dot me do dis zo great distress und misfortune has brought?"'

'But you said that, sir,' interrupted Binns.

'Jah, ah! Krite droo, my liddle vellow; krite droo. I did id zay, but he my vorts did eggo.'

'Why on earth did he do that, sir?' asked Binns.

Herr Steingruber was not equal to explaining. After all, it was Fritz's affair, not his.

'He zay,' resumed the Herr – 'und id is dis dot I ask you zo garefully do marg Pellamy – he zay, "I vos do dis zad ztate of boverty und zorrow reduced by der vact dot in my youth I my boog-worg und language-studies neglected!" Zo!'

He stopped, and eyed his class inquiringly through his spectacles, as who should say, 'What do you think of that for an awful warning?'

But the interest of the class was centred, not on the moral

of the story, but on the subsequent adventures of Fritz. What happened to him? That was what they wanted to know. Did he go on selling collar-studs? Did Herr Steingruber take him off and give him a lunch? Did he do anything for him? Did he buy a toy? Or a stud? Questions rained from all parts of the room.

They were interrupted by Tommy standing up, with his hand pressed to his forehead and a look of pain on his face.

'Might I leave the room, sir?' he asked. 'I am not feeling very well. Neuralgia, sir.'

The kind-hearted Herr was all sympathy.

'Zo, zo,' he said. 'Zertainly – py all means. A liddle vresh air berhaps, or a vew minutes' rest by yourself guietly. Go, my liddle vellow, und redurn vhen you are petter.'

Tommy thanked him, and left the room in a subdued way. When he had shut the door, however, nobody would have taken him for an invalid. His face cleared, and he began to run. He galloped into the house. There seemed to be nobody about. He made his way noiselessly down the passage to Mr Spinder's study.

Mr Spinder, having ascertained beyond any possibility of doubt that the stone was gone, left the bookshelf, and seated himself limply in a chair. The shock had completely unmanned him. He had braced himself up to face what he knew would be the extreme danger of his position now that the mysterious band which was working to get the stone knew that he had it; but this totally unexpected blow temporarily shattered him. For the moment he was a beaten man. All the iron determination which had carried him so successfully through his interview with Ferris had been shaken out of him. His face, as he sat, looked years older. It was drawn and haggard. His fingers plucked feebly at the arm of the chair.

Gradually his fine brain reasserted itself. The dull stupor left him. He could think coherently now.

Who could have stolen the stone?

It was a theft that could not possibly have been the result of an accidental discovery. Nobody could have found the stone unless he had known where to look. Even the removal of the book would have been insufficient to put a searcher on the track unless he had happened to know that what he sought was there, for the hiding-place was invisible. This narrowed the search down to those people who could possibly have known that the stone was in his room. And who did? That this was not the work of the gang, of which Ferris was the representative, he was certain. He knew that Ferris had been genuine in his offers. It must be some independent person, working in opposition both to himself and the Ferris party.

Instantly his mind turned to Jimmy Stewart. As far as he knew – for when he found them fighting in his study he had put Sam Burrows and Marshall down as members of the same gang who had fallen out – as far as he knew, Jimmy was the only person outside Ferris's party who was aware that the stone was in his possession. Jimmy had actually seen him handling it, and it was to Jimmy that it had belonged in the first instance. He did not suppose that Jimmy knew the real value of the stone, but it had been plain that he regarded it as a treasured possession, and would make all possible efforts to recover it. His suspicions centred on Jimmy.

But then there was the objection that Jimmy must have been in school at the time of the robbery. Roughly speaking, the stone must have been taken between eleven and half-past twelve that morning.

Still, he decided to question him.

He did so as he was going in to afternoon school.

'Stewart!'

'Yes, sir.'

'Where were you this morning between eleven and one?'

'I was in school, sir.'

'The whole time?'

'Yes, sir.'

'Who was teaching you?'

'Herr Steingruber, sir,' said Jimmy shortly. He objected to having his word doubted at any time, especially by a man whom he knew to be a thief.

'Very good, Stewart.'

Mr Spinder walked off.

'What's up now, I wonder?' thought Jimmy, as he went into school.

At the conclusion of the afternoon's work Mr Spinder approached Herr Steingruber.

'Ach, my Sbinder,' said the Herr jovially. He was always in a good temper, especially at the end of the day's work.

'I wanted to ask you, Steingruber, if Stewart was in your class-room all the time between eleven and half-past twelve this morning.'

'Sdeward! Jah, zo. He vas.'

'The whole time? He did not leave the room even for a few minutes?'

'No. Der liddle vellow was in his sead from peginning to end of der lesson. It vos der poy Armsdrong who did der room on aggount of a zo zudden addack of illness leave.'

Mr Spinder started. Armstrong! Jimmy's closest friend. Who more likely than he to be chosen by Jimmy as a confidant in this affair? Probably they had talked it over together, and come to the conclusion that Tommy had better take the stone, seeing that Jimmy would occur to Mr Spinder at once as the probable thief. And Armstrong had been out of the room during the morning's lesson.

'How long was Armstrong away?'

'Aboud vive minutes. Berhaps less. He did ad der end of dot dime redurn, zaying dot he had bathed his vorehead und did moch bedder feel.'

'Bathed his forehead. Why?'

'Do relieve der keen neuralgia bangs which did bain him.'

'Neuralgia!'

'Jah, zo. It vos of der neuralgia dot der liddle vellow did gomblain.'

That settled the matter as far as Mr Spinder was concerned. He knew that convenient neuralgia, which was so much better at the end of five minutes. Five minutes! It was all that Tommy would need to enable him to go to the study, take the stone, and return.

He was satisfied now that it was Tommy who had taken it. The only question now was, how to recover it from him. In a way, the problem which faced Mr Spinder was almost as hard as that which had faced Jimmy before. A master could not go to a boy's room and search it whenever he pleased without due reason. He would have to find some excuse.

But what? That was the difficulty. There seemed to be no reason under the sun why he should demand the keys of Tommy's box and ransack it from top to bottom. Boys had their rights, and he knew enough of Tommy to know that he would exercise his to the utmost. If he went to Tommy now, and demanded his keys, Tommy would refuse to give them up. And if he carried the matter to the headmaster, the latter, unless Mr Spinder could produce some adequate reason why he asked to search, would certainly decide in favour of Tommy, and probably read the housemaster a lecture on the limitations of his authority.

Mr Spinder was undeniably baffled. He could see no way out of the tangle.

He wandered out into the playground to think the thing out in the open air. It was dusk by this time, for the evenings were beginning to draw in rapidly.

It was at this point that his luck turned. Wandering slowly in the direction of the gymnasium, he turned the corner of that building, intending to skirt round it and come back the way he had gone. Hardly, however, had he turned the corner when a familiar smell came to his nostrils. The smell of tobacco. At the same moment a faint groan reached his ears. Somebody was smoking under the sheltering wall of the gymnasium, and, to judge from the sounds, it was evidently doing him no good.

Mr Spinder crept stealthily forward. The smoker, however, showed no signs of retreating. When Mr Spinder's grasp fell on a limp arm, the captive scarcely stirred. Mr Spinder shook the arm. Another groan was the only answer.

'Who are you?' demanded the master. 'What are you doing here?'

'Hon'ble sir,' moaned a feeble voice, '*Peccavi*. I am in *articulo mortis* and the utter wreck. Distinguished and benevolent mister, bring the doctor. My last moments are arriving with rapidity of greased lighting-flash.'

Mr Spinder struck a match. It blazed up in the damp air. Against the gymnasium wall was seated Ram, his forehead beaded with perspiration and his face a sickly green. In one hand the stump of a cigar was tightly clutched.

'What does all this mean?' thundered Mr Spinder.

'Benevolent sir,' said Ram feebly, 'do not continue to shake me, or – hoity, toity! – who knows what may not happen? I—'

The warning was too late! Without entering into painful details, one may say that the warning justified itself almost immediately by fact. Mr Spinder waited grimly till all was over.

'Go into the house at once,' he said. 'You will hear more of this.'

'Spare me, benevolent sir,' moaned the sufferer. 'I am the worm.'

'Go in,' said Mr Spinder.

Ram moved painfully off towards the house.

Mr Spinder stood where he was, thinking. Then he started.

In a flash he saw that luck had played into his hands. He had caught one of the boys in his house smoking. Nothing could be more natural or praiseworthy than that he should at once institute a general search through all the boxes in the house. It would be like fishing with a drag-net. He was bound to find the stone. He hurried back to the house, overtaking Ram on the way. Ram, to quote the poem, was 'remote, unfriended, melancholy, slow.' He was dragging himself along, wishing in a sort of general way that he had never been born, and particularly that he had never been seized with the idea of smoking a cigar.

In the study which he shared with Jimmy, meanwhile, Tommy was seated in the only comfortable chair, gazing at something small and blue that lay in the palm of his hand. He was feeling like a successful detective. Alone and unaided, he had tracked down the stone and recovered it. He was now waiting for Jimmy to come in, to show it to him.

He heard a footstep on the stairs, and got up. No, that could not be Jimmy. The step was not his. It was somebody else's, somebody who—

'Spinder, by Jove!' thought Tommy, with a start.

The next moment the door burst open. He was quite right. His visitor was Mr Spinder!

Tommy rose politely as the door opened. Mr Spinder closed the door behind him.

'Armstrong,' he said abruptly, 'I intend to search this study.'

Tommy raised his eyebrows, but said nothing.

'I have reason to believe,' continued the master, 'that a great deal of smoking is going on in the house. I have this very evening found' – here he gave Ram's full name, which, owing to pressure of space, must be omitted; it was the sort of name that covered nearly the whole of one line on a sheet of foolscap when Ram wrote exercises – 'in the act of smoking a large cigar.'

A faint smile appeared on Tommy's face for a brief instant. The idea of Ram smoking a cigar, and the probable result of such a feat, amused him. The smile quickly vanished. He made no spoken comment on the news.

'I have determined,' said Mr Spinder, 'to institute a personal search through the boxes of every boy in the house. I will not have these breaches of important school rules. I don't say that I suspect you or anyone else of having tobacco, but I am resolved to pay no attention to anyone's word, but to make a thorough search on my own account. Ah, Stewart!'

Jimmy had entered during the conclusion of this speech.

'Yes, sir,' said Jimmy.

'I was informing Armstrong that I was about to search this

study thoroughly, to satisfy myself that there is no tobacco concealed here.'

'We haven't any, sir,' said Jimmy.

'I do not wish to hear any statement from you. I intend to satisfy myself by searching. Kindly turn out your pockets, both of you.'

Jimmy and Tommy, the former furious, the latter apparently resigned, proceeded to empty their pockets on to the table. It was a miscellaneous collection that met Mr Spinder's eyes – knives, string, a bag of chocolates, another of jujubes, letters, a screw, two cold roast chestnuts. Everything under the sun, in fact, except the blue stone.

Mr Spinder eyed the collection sourly, and, motioning to them to replace the things, proceeded to make a search round the study. There was not a great deal of cover for the stone to hide in, and he had soon exhausted all the possible places. He turned to the two boys.

'You have boxes?' he said.

'Downstairs, sir,' said Jimmy.

'Give me your keys. Thank you. I will return them to you after I have finished with the boxes.'

He left the room.

Jimmy turned to Tommy.

'What on earth's the matter with him?' he asked. 'Why should he suddenly take it into his head that we are keeping baccy up here?'

Tommy was rolling in a chair with silent laughter.

'You chump!' he said at length. 'Couldn't you spot his game? He was looking for the stone. The baccy was only a bluff to give him an excuse for routing round this place. He-he-ha-ha! – he caught old – old Ram smoking a whacking big cigar this evening.'

Jimmy grinned.

'No!' he said.

'Fact! By Jove, I wish I'd seen him. What an ass old Ram is! I expect he was as sick as a cat.'

'But what did you mean about the stone? Why should Spinder be looking for it?'

'It's gone from his study.'

'Gone! How do you know?'

'Because,' said Tommy calmly, opening his mouth and taking something out, 'here it is!'

He extended his hand with the stone in it. Jimmy stared at it as if it had been some new and hitherto undiscovered animal. The surprise of the thing deprived him of the power of speech.

'How did you get it?' he almost whispered at last.

'When I left the room during old Steingruber's lesson. I shammed ill on purpose to get a chance of slipping out. I knew that during school hours was the only chance I should get of being in Spinder's study without him coming and interrupting. I knew exactly where to look. I'd felt the thing when I looked before. So I nipped across and had it out and got back to the class-room in under five minutes.'

'Tommy, you're a marvel!'

'I have a big brain,' admitted Tommy complacently. 'A very big brain. Sometimes I wonder if it's quite healthy. I suppose old Steingruber must have told him I was out of the room during the morning, and that sent him buzzing up here. Well, here it is. Now, what are we to do with it? It won't be safe to keep it up here or down in either of our boxes. There's no knowing when he may not take it into his head to have another search. What's to be done?'

Jimmy produced a letter from his pocket.

'We shan't have it on our hands long,' he said. 'That's one comfort. This is a letter from my father. It arrived just now. He's back.'

'Good business. Where is he?'

'That's just what I don't know,' said Jimmy ruefully.

'Don't know? Why, where does he write from?'

'From a hotel at Southampton. But he says he's leaving there the same night and going to London. And he doesn't say where he'll be in London. Says he'll write again when he gets there. So we shall have to wait till he does, I suppose.'

'I suppose so. Still, we've got the stone. That's the great thing. Now where shall we hide it?'

Jimmy reflected.

'No good in our dormitory anywhere, I suppose?'

Tommy shook his head.

'Not a bit. He might easily look there. What we must do is to find some place that he can't possibly think of. And it must be a place, of course, that we can get at in a jiffy whenever we want to. Dash it, I wish your pater had given you his London address. Hasn't he got a club?'

'Yes. But I'm blowed if I know which it is.'

'I wish we could find Sam. I wonder where the dickens he is.'

'It's a rum business, isn't it?' said Jimmy. 'Here we are, with the stone, simply waiting to hand it over, and there's nobody to give it to. It's a bit sickening.'

Tommy looked curiously at the stone.

'I wonder,' he said, 'what the thing really is. Why is everyone so keen on getting hold of it? How does your father come to be mixed up with it? And why is it that Spinder knows all about it? He evidently thinks it's worth having, doesn't he?'

'I suppose we shall know soon. I wish we knew where Sam was.'

'It's Indian, I should say. I wonder if Ram would know

anything about it. By the way, I must go down and see Ram. He seems to have been having a stormy time.'

'Don't say anything to him about the stone.'

'Rather not.'

'Oh, talking of Ram reminds me. I never mended that bicycle of his. I promised to. After he had that smash, you know. There's nothing much wrong with it. It won't take me a minute. I'll go and do it now, I think, and get it over.'

'I'll come and help.'

They went downstairs to the back of the house, where the bicycles were kept. Ram's injured machine was leaning forlornly against the wall. Jimmy took out the spanner and got to work. Tommy looked on, which was his notion of helping.

Suddenly Tommy uttered an exclamation.

'By Jove! I've got it!' he cried.

'What's that?' asked Jimmy, looking up.

'Look. Which is your bike?'

'The one over there.'

'The one with the dented mudguards?'

Jimmy nodded.

'Observe,' said Tommy. 'There's no one about, is there?'

He went to the door and looked. The place was empty.

'Now,' he said.

He took the bicycle, and began twisting the tortoiseshell at the end of the handle-bar. It came away in his hand, leaving the bare steel.

'Hollow, you observe,' said Tommy. 'Now we wrap him up neatly in a piece of paper' – he produced the stone, and suited the action to the word – 'shove him in here' – he pushed the little parcel into the tortoiseshell cover – 'and then put the whole thing back. How's that? It doesn't go on quite so far as it should, but nobody's likely to notice that. After all, you won't be lending your bike to Spinder, I suppose. There!'

Jimmy rose, and inspected the result.

'That's good,' he said, with approval. 'That's a good idea.'

'My brain,' said Tommy, 'is something colossal. I often think of charging a small fee for talking to people. Let's be going upstairs, shall we? The stone's as safe as houses now.'

On the stairs they met Mr Spinder.

'Where have you been?' he inquired irritably. He had been searching vigorously ever since he had left them, with absolutely no result. He had not even found tobacco, which would have been better than nothing. Ram's cigar seemed to be the sole specimen of the world's tobacco industries at present within the walls of Marleigh.

'Where have you been?' he said. 'I went to your study, but you were not there. I have left your keys on the table.'

'Thank you, sir,' said Tommy politely. 'We have been downstairs mending Ram's bicycle. He had a spill riding home after the football match, and injured it a little.'

'Well, well, either go up to your study again or to the dayroom. I cannot have you wandering about like this all over the house.'

'Yes, sir,' said Tommy.

They walked on.

'For choice,' said Tommy, 'give me the dayroom. It is nice and quiet in our study, but I want to see Ram. I should think he must be worth seeing after that cigar. Poor old Spinder!'

If he could have seen Mr Spinder at that moment he would have felt that his pity was no more than was needed. The housemaster was sitting at his study table, staring blankly before him, seeing nothing. The unexpected turn the game had taken had had its effect on Mr Spinder.

It takes very little to upset the best-laid plans. In theory the stone was perfectly safe in the handle-bar of Jimmy's bicycle. Nobody could possibly guess that it was there. In theory the handle-bar was an ideal retreat.

But all the theoretical value of the hiding-place was totally destroyed by the simple fact that Herr Steingruber was engaged to be married to a girl in his native town of Munich.

There does not seem much connection at first sight between the two things. Yet it undoubtedly existed.

Miss Gretchen Steidl, of Munich, was a young lady with expectations. When an uncle died, she would be comfortably situated. Till that melancholy event she kept the wolf from the door by teaching the alphabet and elementary drawing to infants in a kindergarten. Herr Hans, meanwhile, separated from her by many miles of sea, taught German to English boys at Marleigh. The parted pair had to console themselves by writing each other long letters.

Now it happened, on the afternoon of this particular day, that Herr Steingruber had spent all the time between lunch and the gathering of darkness on the links. His play had not improved to any great extent since his first introduction to the game, but his enthusiasm had increased wonderfully. He spent the afternoon smiting furiously, sometimes at the air, sometimes at the turf, less frequently at the ball. The result of all this energy was that when he arrived home and had had his tea he felt thoroughly tired. Comfortably so, and extremely sleepy. After a pipe in an armchair before the fire he had fallen sound asleep, and only awoke in time for dinner. After dinner he still felt drowsy. He sat in his chair smoking, till he suddenly remembered with a start that he had not written to his Gretchen.

This was a duty that had to be attended to at once. Yawning hugely, he stretched himself and went to the table. His letters to Gretchen always took him a long time to write. It was not till half-past nine that he had finished. Reading the letter over and dreaming of the day when they should retire together to Munich on the money of the uncle, who still clung obstinately to life, and spend their time listening to Wagner, occupied time till twenty minutes to ten. Then he stamped the letter, and went to the door.

A housemaid was passing at the moment.

'Ach!' said Herr Steingruber, 'vill you dis ledder do der post-poy give, vor do dake do der bost?'

'Lor, sir,' said the housemaid, 'he's been gone this half-hour.'

It was the boot-boy's duty to collect the letters of the house and bicycle to the village post-office with them. The post-office was three miles from the school, and letters had to be in the box by ten o'clock. As a rule, he did not start on his journey till about half-past nine; but tonight, wishing to get back early in time to continue his acquaintance with a paper-covered book, which he had bought, entitled 'Black Bill of the Mountains, or the Scourge of California,' he had left early.

'Himmel!' was Herr Steingruber's reply to this bad news. 'I haf der bost missed.'

Herr Steingruber was a favourite with the servants at the

school, partly because he was exceedingly free with his money, and partly because he was unvaryingly good-tempered and always spoke pleasantly to them. This was the reason why the house-maid, instead of passing on and thinking no more about the matter, stopped sympathetically and tried to be helpful.

'It's only a quarter to the hour, sir,' she said. 'If you'd got a bicycle, sir—'

'Alas! I no bicygle haf,' sighed the Herr.

'Or if one of the young gentlemen could go—'

'Ach, no, dey are to der house by der log-ub rule gonfined. Do sdray and move out of der house ad der hour of ten o'glog, dot vas do der poys vorpidden. But – ach! I haf id got, I haf id got! I vill der picygle of der boy porrow, and myself on id do der host wit der greatest sbeed hurry. Dthangk you, you haf do me der idea given.'

To rush to the basement where the bicycles were kept took Herr Steingruber under a minute. It was just a quarter to ten when he wheeled his machine out of a side gate into the road, mounted, and began to pedal.

Or, rather, not his machine, but Jimmy's. For the Herr, faced with the task of choosing between a dozen bicycles, had selected Jimmy's.

This he did principally because the seat was a good deal higher than the seats on the other machines. Jimmy always liked a high seat.

The road to the village was uphill for a quarter of a mile, downhill for two miles, and level for about three-quarters of a mile. The Herr was slightly behind the clock and very much out of breath when he arrived at the top of the first incline, but he made up for lost time on the downward slope. Free-wheeling, he moved along at a capital pace, and, having recovered his breath during the two miles of coasting, he was able to finish up on the flat with a fine spurt, which landed him, moist but triumphant, at the post-office with a good two and a half minutes in hand.

'Ach!' he grunted with placid triumph. 'Vigtory! I haf id on mein head done.'

He was very pleased with himself indeed. He felt that he had carried through a difficult business with skill and precision. Gretchen would be pleased to get that letter. She would have been bitterly disappointed if none had arrived.

The Herr leaped on to Jimmy's bicycle, and began to pedal slowly homewards, thinking of Miss Steidl and Munich, and everything except the fact that he was on a bicycle. His afternoon's golf and the brisk ride to the post had left him in that curiously dreamy state, which is often the result of physical fatigue. He had to tramp up the last mile of the hill before reaching the incline that led to the school gates; and by the time the hill ceased, and he was able to mount his machine again, all he wanted was to free-wheel dreamily, thinking of her.

This he did. In fact, he lost himself to such an extent in his thoughts that the first intimation he had that he was still a dweller in the practical, everyday world, bicycling in the dark down a steepish incline, was the colliding of his front wheel with something hard and unyielding. The fact was, that the Herr, who never used the main entrance to the school ground except in daylight when the gate was wide open, had completely forgotten that there was a gate there at all. The consequence was that, wrapped in thought, he charged into it without the slightest slackening of speed, and only escaped an uncommonly nasty accident by mere good luck. He shot off, but fortunately to one side, not straight over the handle-bars; so that, instead of dashing against the iron bars, he only staggered and sat down rather hard in the road, getting off with a severe shaking instead of broken bones.

The bicycle, having rammed the gate, fell over with a great clatter and a noisy ring of the bell.

'Who in the world's that?' asked a voice from the other side of the gate.

Herr Steingruber did not reply for a moment. He was not at all satisfied at first that it *was* anybody in the world. He had a strong disposition to think that he was dead. Then his head began to clear, and he rose with a groan.

'Who's that?' said the voice again, sharply.

'Ach! my Spinder,' said the Herr, recognising the accents, 'I am moch shagen.'

'Is that you, Steingruber? What has happened?'

'I haf a bicygle aggident had.'

'Are you hurt?'

'I am shagen, moch shagen.'

'Can you walk?'

'Jah! I can walg. But der bicygle, he is all do bieces smashed. And he vos not mine, but do one of der liddle vellows did belong.'

'Come round to the small gate. Carry the bicycle if you can't wheel it. I can't let you in here. The porter has the keys.'

With many groans the Herr made his way to the little gate, carrying the bicycle. It was impossible to wheel it. The front spokes were twisted and broken, and he could feel that the handle-bar was injured, too.

Mr Spinder met him at the gate, and helped to convey the machine to where there was light enough to examine it.

'H'm!' said Mr Spinder. 'You've certainly done the machine no good.'

'Der damage I vill vrom my own burse devray.'

'Whose bicycle is it?'

'Dot I do nod know. I vos in a hurry to gatch der bost, and I him ad random dook.'

Mr Spinder was looking at the machine.

'I think it must be Stewart's,' he said. 'I have noticed that he rides with his saddle particularly high. What on earth is this?'

He was looking at the handle-bar. The tortoiseshell at the end was split and gaping, and through the rents protruded paper.

'What do they want to put paper in there for, I wonder,' said Mr Spinder.

Herr Steingruber merely groaned. An injudicious movement had caused a twinge to pass through his aching bones.

Mr Spinder was twisting the tortoiseshell. It came off in his hand. All at once, as he looked at it, he became rigid. The hand which held it shook.

'If I were you,' he said to Herr Steingruber, in a curiously strained voice, 'I should go and change your clothes and lie down. You want a rest. Better take a stiff brandy and soda. You're shaken.'

'Jah, zo! I am shagen, moch shagen.'

'Go along, then. You'll find brandy and soda in my room. If not, ring and ask for it.'

'Dthangks, dthangks,' murmured the Herr, and dragged himself from the room.

When he had gone, Mr Spinder removed from the handle-bar the paper and what it contained. Then he replaced the paper very carefully, and screwed on the tortoiseshell once more.

There was a smile on his thin lips as he went to the bell and pressed it.

'Send Master Stewart here,' he said, when the servant appeared.

Jimmy was reading a book when the summons came, with the comfortable feeling that his troubles were over, and that he had now nothing to worry about.

'What on earth does he want me for? I wonder,' he grumbled, getting up.

'Better go and see,' suggested Tommy, who was binding a cricket bat. 'And don't forget to give him my love. Tell him that I'm always thinking of him.'

Jimmy went, and found the housemaster waiting in the hall, holding the bicycle.

His first thought was that Mr Spinder, suspecting the presence of the stone in the bicycle, had been exploring with a pick-axe. The machine certainly looked a pretty bad wreck.

'Oh, Stewart,' said Mr Spinder, 'this is your bicycle, I think?'

'Yes, sir.'

'I am afraid there has been an accident. Herr Steingruber was in a hurry to catch the post, and took the first bicycle which came to hand. It, unfortunately, happened to be yours. He ran into the gate, and has, I am afraid, damaged the machine a good deal. He will, of course, pay for the repairs. Will you take it down into the basement, please?'

Jimmy's first glance, when the machine was in his hands, was for the handle-bar. It was badly smashed. He noticed the paper peeping out at one of the cracks. A near shave, he thought. Spinder might have seen it, and wondered what it was.

It was not till he was down in the basement, and had time to look more closely, that he discovered his loss. The paper was there, but the stone had disappeared.

He rushed up to the study, where Tommy was still sitting binding his bat.

'Well,' said Tommy, without looking up, 'what did he want you for?'

'Tommy,' cried Jimmy, 'it's gone. The stone's gone.'

'What! How could it have gone? Who would think of looking there? What do you mean?'

Jimmy related what had happened. Tommy whistled softly.

'What frightful luck!' he said.

'What are we to do?'

'That's rather a problem. You're certain the stone really isn't there? Hasn't got shoved up into the handle-bar?'

'Absolutely. The paper you wrapped it in is still there. Spinder must have seen it, and suspected something, and put back the paper after he'd got the stone. What shall we do?'

'We must think this out.'

'We're exactly where we were before you got the thing from the bookshelf.'

Tommy shook his head.

'We aren't,' he said, 'by a long way. Not by a very long way, indeed. Don't you see that, before this happened, Spinder had no notion that we knew anything about the bookcase? He was simply watching out for Ferris and his gang. He didn't think that we were in the hunt at all, especially me. Now he's on his guard. He won't trust to the bookcase again. He'll shove the bally stone somewhere else. Probably he'll keep it on him, and sleep with it under his pillow. My word, this is a pretty tough nut. What a fool old Steingruber was to go charging into the gate like that. And what rotten luck. I'm blowed if I know what we're going to do now.'

The game certainly seemed very much in Mr Spinder's hands. They could hardly hope to discover the next hiding-place in which he might place the stone, even if he did not make it absolutely secure from them by keeping it always on his person.

'The only thing is, though,' said Tommy, 'he might be afraid to carry it about with him, in case Ferris or Marshall got hold of him. Not that that helps us much. If you ask me, I think we're done. We've shot our bolt. All we can do is to tell your pater who's got the stone, and let him have a try at getting it.'

The next day passed, and the next, but still they were as far from hitting on any solution of the difficulty.

Herr Steingruber met Jimmy, and was full of apologies.

'More zorry dan I gan eggsbress, my liddle Sdewart,' he said, 'am I dot dis should have oggurred. I do myself did zay: "I must der bost vor do zend my ledder do Germany gatch, und der is no dime to zee der liddle vellows, und vor der loan of der bicygle ask. Bot dey would, I am sure, wit gladness und readiness der bicygle lend, zo I will id dake." Bot, alas! Garelessly und wit' der absend mind did I dowards der gade ride, und grash! Dere vos I, moch shagen, on der ground, und der bicygle, he vos moch injured. Bot do not rebine, my liddle vellow, vor I vill myself all der exbenses of der mending upon myself dake, und in a vew days, a very vew days, back gom der bicygle as goot as new, and you are once again wit id habby. Zo!'

Jimmy thanked him, and said politely that the smash-up did not matter a bit; but that was far from being what he really thought. He had had another letter from his father, written from the Grand Hotel in London, in which the Colonel said that he was motoring down on the following Wednesday, and would put up for the night at the Crown Hotel in the village. It was there that the Colonel always stayed when he visited Jimmy at Marleigh. The Crown was a comfortable inn of the old-fashioned country sort, and Jimmy had had some very pleasant meals there with his father in the days before his life became complicated by the stone and the responsibilities it brought with it.

The Colonel added that he would be breakfasting on the Thursday morning at eight o'clock, as he had to return to London on some business which, though not extremely important, might as well be attended to and disposed of. He hoped to see Jimmy at that meal, and had not forgotten that Jimmy had a preference for scrambled eggs on toast.

It was on the afternoon of this day that Jimmy met Sam again. Sam had been waiting near the school gates for him to come out.

Jimmy put him in possession of the fact of the case as shortly as he could, and Sam, like Tommy, was of opinion that the position was a difficult one.

'And father's coming down tomorrow,' said Jimmy.

'What, the Colonel! That's good news. Maybe he'll see a way out of this.'

Sam's confidence in the ability of his old officer to cope with any situation, however difficult, was immense. He had been with Colonel Stewart in some very tight corners indeed, and had that faith in him which the officers of our Indian army inspire in their men.

'But before he comes,' said Sam, 'I think as how you might have another try for the stone. Couldn't you get into the room again, and look about?'

'It's no good trying that game now, Sam, or I'd do it like a shot. Spinder always locks his door at night now. We tried to get in the other night, just before Tommy got hold of the stone, and we found we couldn't.'

Sam fumbled in his pocket.

'We'll soon get over that,' he said. 'See here, this is one of those skeleton keys.'

'By Jove! The one you were opening the drawers of his desk with that night you and Marshall fought. Let's have it.'

'If the stone's locked up anywhere in 'is room – and it might be – you'll soon have it out with that.'

'Thanks, Sam. That's splendid. I think you'd better go to the Crown, and meet father when he arrives, and tell him all about this. I'll be trying for the stone.'

Jimmy went back, and found Tommy.

'It's all right about getting into Spinder's study,' he said. 'Sam Burrows has given me a skeleton key. It'll unlock anything. We'll go down tonight.'

'Not tonight,' said Tommy.

'Why not?'

'I've an idea. I'm pretty certain Spinder has got that stone on him at present. I think he'd carry it about with him for a day or two till he could think of somewhere to hide it. But I think he's bound to hide it in the end, so as to run no risk of being collared with it on him. After a bit he won't think much of our chances of getting the thing. He'll think that a locked door is enough to keep us out. And then he'll shove it back in its old place behind the books. Because, you see, except for us that's a ripping place for it. The Ferris gang can't know of it. They might break in and search for hours without finding anything. And he won't be afraid of us. All he'll do, by way of choking us off, is to keep the door locked all day instead of only at night. So we'll give him another day. Then we'll nip down tomorrow night and see what happens.'

'All right. Sam's going to wait at the Crown for my pater, and tell him all about what's been happening.'

'Just as well,' said Tommy. 'He couldn't do any good by hanging round here. This job can only be tackled from inside the house. Tomorrow night, then. And I only hope we have some luck!'

It was not with any very great feeling of hopefulness that Jimmy accompanied Tommy over the difficult route which lay between them and Mr Spinder's study on the following night. Tommy's theory that the master would look on them as out of the battle, and feel that the old hiding-place behind the books was as good as any others, was not so sound as it had seemed on first sight. Of course, Mr Spinder might do that, but Jimmy was not very hopeful. He knew the housemaster too well to believe that he would be capable of such carelessness and want of resource. However, he did not tell Tommy that this was his view. The latter was full of confidence, and it seemed a pity to discourage him.

They stole downstairs in their gymnasium shoes, pausing every now and then to listen. No sound came to their ears. The house seemed asleep.

They could find their way to Mr Spinder's study in the dark easily now.

'Got the key?' whispered Tommy.

Jimmy handed it to him. Before trying to find the lock, Tommy turned the handle, more from force of habit than because he expected any result from the action. To his surprise, at first, and then to his horror, he found that the door was not locked. To his horror, because the push which opened the door also let loose a stream of light, which darted out into the passage. The room, instead of being dark and empty, was lit up.

Was it occupied? That was the question which the two boys asked themselves, as they stood there paralysed, Tommy still holding the handle. Every moment they expected to hear a sharp voice cry, 'Who is that?' from inside the room. Each second that passed seemed like an hour, till at length, reassured by the silence, Tommy pushed the door still further open, and looked in.

There was nobody in the room. But there were plenty of signs that somebody had been there only a short time before. A great book was open on the desk, and a cigar smouldered on an ashtray beside it.

Tommy looked at Jimmy, and Jimmy looked blankly at Tommy.

'We'd better be getting back,' said Jimmy.

'And jolly quick, too, or we shall be caught here. He'll probably be back in a minute. I can't think why we didn't meet him.'

'This is no place for us,' agreed Tommy. 'What on earth is he doing up so late? Shift ho, I think!'

They were on the point of retracing their steps down the corridor when Tommy clutched Jimmy by the arm.

'Listen!' Somebody was coming down the stairs.

Tommy was a man of action.

'In here! Quick!' he whispered.

They were in the study, and had closed the door behind them before the man on the stairs could turn the corner. Their old ally, the piano, was standing in the corner it had always occupied.

'In there,' said Tommy. 'Look sharp.'

Jimmy scrambled behind the piano. Tommy followed him.

Just as they had settled themselves down as comfortably as was possible, the door opened, and somebody walked across to the writing-table and sat down. From the smell of smoke it was evident that he had continued his cigar at the point where he had left off.

Then ensued the weariest period of waiting which either of the two boys had ever experienced, rendered even more wearisome than it might have been by the fact that only with the utmost caution could they move their limbs. They began to feel cramped and stiff, but still the master sat where he was. They heard him throw away his cigar and light another. Once there came the swish of soda-water into a glass. At intervals there was the rustling sound of the pages of the big book being turned. Jimmy and Tommy came ruefully to the conclusion that Mr Spinder had made himself comfortable, and got hold of a book which interested him, and intended to make a night of it. They both wondered dismally how they would feel after an hour or so of waiting.

Things must have gone on like this for about half an hour, when a very faint sound made itself heard. Both boys had heard it before, on that memorable night when Sam and Marshall had fought on the floor in this same room. It was the sound of a diamond on glass. Somebody was cutting out a pane.

The curtains were drawn in front of the window, so that nobody outside could tell that there was anyone in the room. The man, whoever he was, had made the same mistake that Jimmy and Tommy had made, in supposing that at such a late hour it was certain that there would be nobody about.

Mr Spinder got up. They heard his chair creak as he rose. The next moment the room was in darkness. The master had switched off the electric light.

The scratching noise continued for a long time, then stopped. There was a soft, a very soft, thud as a foot touched the carpet, and a momentary rustle as the curtains were pushed back. Tommy gripped Jimmy's arm excitedly. What was going to happen? They wondered that Mr Spinder could not hear their hearts thumping.

The visitor breathed a long, soft breath. Then he uttered a gasping curse, for the room was suddenly flooded with light again, and the dry, hard voice of Mr Spinder spoke.

'Good evening,' he said. 'Rather an unceremonious mode of entry, is it not? The last time I had the honour of a visit from you, you came and left by the front door quite in the orthodox style. Is there anything I can do for you? I take it that such a late call as this must be a business visit.'

The other man laughed.

'You've got me,' he said. 'Don't let that gun go off.'

'Ferris,' whispered Jimmy in Tommy's ear.

What happened after that was so rapid that Tommy could not follow it. He saw Ferris dip languidly in the side pocket of his coat, and draw out a handkerchief. Then suddenly the scene changed to one of noise and movement. He saw Ferris suddenly open and shoot forward his hand. What left it he could not see, but he heard Mr Spinder utter a piercing cry of agony, and, springing from his seat, stagger about the room. His head and shoulders appeared above the level of the piano, swaying. He had dropped the revolver, and was covering his face with both hands. He plunged heavily against the piano, causing it to rock. Then there came the sound of a blow being struck, followed by a crash, as the housemaster's body fell heavily to the ground.

They could hear Ferris's quick breathing, as he knelt beside the body and searched for the stone with feverish haste. From far away in the other part of the house came the noise of voices and running footsteps. Mr Spinder's cry had roused the house.

Ferris muttered oaths as he searched. He darted to the door and locked it. As he did so running footsteps made themselves heard.

'Mr Spinder!' cried a voice.

There followed a rapping of knuckles on the panels.

'Mr Spinder!'

Ferris was tearing the prostrate man's clothes in his haste.

'Come on!' shouted Jimmy to Tommy.

They sprang up.

At the same moment Ferris leaped to his feet with a cry of triumph, holding something aloft in his hand. For a moment he stood there, staring at them, while the panels of the door splintered beneath the blows from outside. Then, leaping to the window, he sprang out.

Jimmy and Tommy followed on his heels. Ferris was running down the road; but he was a stout man, and Jimmy and Tommy, helped by their condition, had begun to overhaul him, when he turned and stopped. There was a flash and a crack. A bullet zipped between the two boys. Another flicked up the dust at their feet. Ferris turned and ran on again.

The two boys redoubled their efforts, but, as they ran, they were aware of a throbbing noise down the road. Ferris heard it, and shouted. An answering shout came from the darkness.

'It's a motor,' gasped Jimmy. 'Quick, or he'll get to it.'

But he had already done so. The throbbing increased in volume, and the black mass began to slide away into the night.

The two boys stood where they were, looking after it. So fixed was their attention that they did not notice that from behind them there was coming the ever-increasing murmur of a second car.

They realised it just in time, and sprang to one side just as the car, with much jarring of brakes, pulled up short.

It was a big car, but there was only one man in it. He seemed irritated.

'What the deuce do you mean by standing out in the middle of the road like that on a dark night?' he shouted over his shoulder.

Jimmy knew the voice.

'Father!' he cried, and dashed towards the car.

'Who on—! Jimmy! whatever are you doing out here at this time of night?'

'Father, catch that motor in front,' gasped Jimmy, clambering on to the seat by Colonel Stewart's side.

'Who's this?'

'That's Tommy. Tommy Armstrong. Nip into the car, Tommy. Do make haste, father, or they'll get away.'

Colonel Stewart was a man who believed in doing a thing first, and asking for explanations afterwards. He released the clutch, and opened the throttle, and the big motor raced away down the road. The noise of the other car could be heard faintly in the distance. By now it must have been half a mile ahead.

'And now,' said Colonel Stewart, 'perhaps you'll kindly explain, my son, why I am risking my neck in this way, and who your friends in the car in front are.'

'Haven't you seen Sam?'

'I have not seen Sam,' said the Colonel politely. 'Who may Sam be?'

'Sam Burrows.'

'Corporal Sam Burrows, who was under me in the Surreys?'

'Yes.'

'And how in the world do you come to be mixed up with Corporal Burrows?'

Jimmy, as briefly and clearly as he could, told his father the whole story from the beginning; how he had met Sam, how Sam had been shot, how the stone had been entrusted to himself, and how it had passed from hand to hand in a sort of hunt-the-slipper fashion, till finally it had been taken by Ferris, who was now, with his accomplices, speeding away into the night at forty miles an hour in the car whose tail-lights they could just see.

The Colonel listened with growing interest.

'You seem to have had a fairly lively term,' he said, when Jimmy had finished. 'What sort of stone was it? Can you describe it?'

'It was a rummy blue stone, with scratches on it. It looked like blue sealing-wax.'

The Colonel took his eyes from the road for a moment, to look at Jimmy with increased interest.

'Blue?' he said. 'Like blue sealing-wax? Can it have been? It must be. But how in the world did Corporal Burrows get hold of it? How big was this stone?'

'About the size of a shilling.'

'What sort of scratches were there on it? Did they look like writing?'

'Yes. In some rum language, though.'

'It must be the same. Good heavens, if they get away with it! We must catch that car if we follow it to the other end of England.'

He opened the throttle still wider. The car seemed to bound over the road, as a racehorse might gallop. Jimmy hung on to the side of his seat with all his might, and Tommy, in the tonneau, was being bumped up and down as if he were the ball in a cup-and-ball game. Jimmy felt very cold. The glass screen broke the force of the wind to a great extent; but it was a chilly night, and he was not dressed for motoring. Tommy was doing better, for he had found a rug on the floor of the car, and was tolerably comfortable in it. The Colonel, muffled to the eyes in a huge coat, and wearing fur gloves, was the best off of the three.

Gradually, however, Jimmy began to forget the cold in the excitement of the chase. The car in front was powerful and speedy, but the Colonel's had the advantage of it.

Little by little the pursuers were gaining. The tail-lights of the other car gleamed quite close now. Jimmy could see the dark figures of the occupants of its tonneau, as they stood up and looked back at the motor that was chasing them. It was evident that they realised now that there was a motive in this pursuit, and that the car behind them was not merely a chance traveller down the same road.

The road was one of those broad, well-laid tracks which the Romans put down in England to be a memorial of themselves to all time. It ran almost straight for mile after mile across the level plain. At intervals a straggling village broke the symmetry of it. Neither car slowed down at these villages. They passed through with a roar and a rattle which probably roused the inhabitants from their slumbers and set them wondering what was happening.

The night was dark but for the rare gleams of a moon which never succeeded in breaking completely through the drifting clouds.

The other car was very close now.

The dark figures were standing up again. Suddenly there was a flash and a report, sounding faintly above the measured roar of the engines. Something struck the woodwork of the glass screen, and sang away into space.

'Hullo!' said Colonel Stewart. 'Revolvers! This won't do. I forgot that they might be armed. We must slow down a bit.'

He closed the throttle slightly, and the other car bounded ahead. A derisive shout came to them like a distant whisper. Jimmy cried out in dismay.

'It's all right,' said the Colonel reassuringly, as he leaned back in his seat. 'They think they've done us, but they haven't. I don't happen to want my paint chipped off with bullets, but I can follow them all night and all day, keeping them in sight. I've enough petrol to last out any car on the road. And when it's daylight they won't be in such a hurry to shoot off revolvers. We can take it easy for a little now.'

'If it wasn't for that revolver we could overhaul them in five minutes,' said Tommy.

'Yes, we— Great Scott!'

The two uttered a simultaneous shout, for the tail-lights of the car they were pursuing seemed to leap into the air. The next moment there was a fearful crash. The lights went out. A great shriek rent the air. Then, save for the mad roaring of the engines, there was silence.

Colonel Stewart threw out his clutch, and applied the brake. The car slowed down, and stopped.

'What's happened? What is it?' cried the two boys, awed by the sense of disaster in the air.

Colonel Stewart drew off his gloves, and got down.

'Stay here,' he said shortly. 'They've had a smash. I am going to look. Stay where you are, you boys. If they are not killed, they may shoot.'

He unscrewed one of the large lamps from the front of the car. The engines of the wrecked motor had stopped now, and all was silence.

He shouted. There was no reply.

He moved cautiously down the road. Jimmy and Tommy

strained their eyes, but could see nothing. Everything was dark and vague. They saw the light of the lamp darting about the road and the ditches on either side. It rested now and then on certain shapeless heaps.

Then the Colonel walked slowly back to them. His face, as he drew near, looked very stern and set.

'Well?' cried both boys in a breath.

The Colonel's voice, when he spoke, was grave.

'One of their wheels came off just as they were rounding a curve. The car is smashed all to pieces. They must have been travelling at over thirty-five miles an hour.'

'And—'

'And the men?' said the Colonel. 'All dead.'

Tommy was scrambling down from the car, but the Colonel ordered him back sharply.

'It's not a fit sight for you,' he said. 'I am used to these things, but it has given me a shock. It is a horrible sight, Jimmy.'

'Yes, father.'

'Which of the men was it that took the stone? There is one who seems to have been an Indian. The other two are un-recognisable. One of them seems to have been a stout man. Was that the thief?'

'Yes. Ferris. That was the man.'

'Wait here. I must go and search him.'

Tommy and Jimmy waited, awed into silence by the sudden tragedy which had chilled the excitement of the chase in them. Both felt a little sick. They had vivid imaginations, and they could picture to themselves what sort of sight it must be at which Colonel Stewart was now looking.

Presently the Colonel came back again.

'Jimmy,' he said huskily, 'you'll find a small flask in the flap on the right-hand door of the tonneau. Hand it to me, will you?'

He took a long drink, and slipped the flask into his pocket. Then he took it out again, and handed it to the boys.

'You had better drink a little,' he said. 'You must be frozen.'

The biting, burning spirit put new life into Jimmy and Tommy. They hated the taste, but as medicine it was wonderful.

'Have you got it, father?' asked Jimmy.

Colonel Stewart held his hand in the glare of the front lamp. In the palm was a small, round object. The boys noticed with a shudder that the hand was wet with something thick and dark.

The Colonel took a rag from under the seat, and wiped his hand.

'We must be getting back to the nearest village,' he said, taking the wheel, 'to tell the police of what has happened.'

The car was turned with some difficulty in the confined space, and they went back along the road till they reached the village through which they had passed ten minutes before. They stopped at the police station. A sleepy constable answered their knock.

'I am Colonel Stewart,' said the Colonel. 'There has been a motor smash down the road.'

The constable blinked sleepily.

'Three men have been killed. One was a burglar escaping from justice.'

The constable's sleepiness left him.

'Burglar, sir!' he repeated. 'Where was the burglary?'

'At Marleigh. We have been pursuing him in my car. He was certainly a burglar, and possibly a murderer as well.'

This finally woke the constable up. He saw himself being promoted for his connection with this affair. Burglary and possibly murder! He must be in this.

'You leave the matter in my 'ands, sir,' he said, as briskly as it is possible for a country policeman to speak. 'About 'ow far down the road? Five or six miles, sir? Right; I'll roust up landlord Smith, of the "King's Head," and get a cart. You'll leave your card, sir, as a matter of form.'

The Colonel handed him his card, and set the car in movement again. It was a very long way back to Marleigh, and both the boys were fast asleep in the tonneau long before they arrived. The stoppage in front of the door awoke them.

Very sleepy, and feeling as if they had not been to bed at all, Jimmy and Tommy dragged themselves up at half-past seven next morning, and made their way, yawning, to the village inn.

The Colonel was not down, and they dozed in armchairs till breakfast and he arrived simultaneously. The Colonel had not turned a hair. His lean, brown face showed no signs of fatigue whatsoever. A life of campaigning and big game shooting leaves a man tough. Colonel Stewart looked as if he had gone to bed at ten o'clock and slept peacefully from the moment his head touched the pillow.

'Well,' he said cheerily, 'and how are you both? No ill effects, eh? Sit down and have some breakfast. You look as if you could hardly keep your eyes open. Tea would be better for you than coffee. Here, waiter, bring some tea. Come along, my boys. It's no good asking me any questions till after breakfast, for I shan't answer them.'

The Colonel ate little but toast for breakfast himself, but he had ordered for the benefit of the two boys a meal such as they had never had before. After the apology for breakfast to which they had grown accustomed under Mr Spinder's rule the present meal seemed too good to be true. Even their curiosity gave way before their determination to make hay while the sun shone. The Colonel had no need to repeat his injunction against questions. Both Jimmy and Tommy were too busy for them.

At last Jimmy leaned back in his chair and said, 'Ah!' Tommy, almost simultaneously, uttered a contented sigh.

'Finished?' said the Colonel, lighting a cheroot.

Jimmy and Tommy nodded.

'And now you want to hear all about it?' Jimmy and Tommy nodded again. There are moments when speech is a nuisance.

'Well, I'll tell you. But let's have everything in its proper order. First your story, then Corporal Burrows', then mine. Burrows will be here soon. Meanwhile, let's have your yarn, Jimmy.'

Jimmy was not feeling in the mood for speech, but he made the necessary effort, and told his father, as briefly as he could, the story of his adventures with the stone; how he had received it from Sam; how Mr Spinder had taken it; and how Marshall and the others had dogged him, thinking it was in his possession.

The Colonel listened attentively.

'You seem to have had a lively term,' he said. 'I suppose,' he added carelessly, 'you realised that there would be a certain amount of danger attached to the possession of the stone when you took it over?'

'I was afraid there might be a bit.'

'But you took it all the same.'

'I thought I might as well,' said Jimmy awkwardly.

Colonel Stewart's eyes flashed with approval. 'Jimmy,' he said quietly, 'you're a brick.' Jimmy blushed to the roots of his hair. He had an overwhelming admiration for his father, and these few words of praise from him were more welcome than a long eulogy from anyone else. He knew that his father was a man who had a high standard, and that he never said very much at any time. That simple remark of the Colonel's was more than enough to reward him for all he had passed through.

'Thanks awfully, father,' he muttered, and there was a silence till a knock at the door made itself heard and Sam Burrows entered. Sam stood stiffly at attention in the presence of the Colonel, and looked as if he were prepared to go on so standing till the end of the interview; but Colonel Stewart motioned him to a seat, gave him one of his cheroots, and ordered beer for him. Sam looked slightly disturbed at this unusual conduct on the part of an officer, but thawed under the influence of the cheroot.

'I missed you last night, Burrows,' said the Colonel. 'I was due to arrive at the inn at about eleven, but I had a couple of punctures.'

'It was lucky you did, father,' said Jimmy. 'We should have been done if you hadn't come by just then. Does Sam know about what happened?'

'Yes. I saw him for a few minutes, when I got back. I told him the main facts. What I want from you now, Burrows, is the story of your dealings with this stone.' He produced the blue stone and laid it beside his plate. They all looked at it with interest. In itself it was an insignificant object, but it had been the cause of many strange happenings.

'Now then, Burrows,' said the Colonel.

Sam took a pull at his mug of beer and began his story.

'I don't rightly know much about the stone, sir,' he said, 'not about why it was so valuable and that. I can only tell you what 'appened to me along of it, and 'ow I got it.'

'That's what I want to know,' said Colonel Stewart. 'I'm going to tell you about the stone when you've finished your story.'

'It was up in Estapore, sir. I was Major Ingram's servant.'

'Major Ingram succeeded me as political agent at Estapore when I went home on leave.'

'Right, sir. I was the Major's servant. One morning he sent for me. "Burrows," he says, "you and me have got to get over to England sharp on a matter of life and death and find Colonel Stewart." "Right, sir," I says. "When do we start?" "In half an hour," says the Major. "Right, sir," I says. We didn't stop to pack and say goodbye to the girls and boys. We just saddled horses and let out as fast as we knew for the railway, which, as you know, sir, is a precious long way off. The Major had told me to keep my eyes skinned and never to let my revolver out of my 'and, and 'e'd do the same. And, my word! it's lucky we didn't take no risks. Night and day, day and night, it was just the same. Somebody was after us. Who it was, was what we didn't bloomin' well know. It wasn't more than once in a blue moon we'd see anybody, but they was sniping us. All the bloomin' time they was sniping us. Sometimes with Mausers, for all the world as if it had been South Africa and the Boers over again, and sometimes with that bloomin' air-gun of theirs, wot laid me out subsequent, as Master Jimmy here knows. We didn't stop to argue about it. We galloped on as fast as our 'orses would let us, down valleys, across rivers, all the bloomin' fun of the fair. Till at last, about one day's easy journey from the rail-head, we get to a Dâk Bungalow. And that was the 'ottest part of the whole entertainment. Knowin' we was pretty nearly 'ome – 'cos, once we was in the train it 'ud be difficult to corner us – they made their big effort. Tried to rush us, the beggars. A dozen of 'em, there was. Either they'd squared the 'ead waiter of the bloomin' Rowton 'Ouse we was in, or scared him. Anyway, he wasn't on the premises. We was all alone with them. There was one blackie wot seemed to be the leader. He came forward to where we'd barricaded ourselves, and he slung a lot of talk at the Major in Hindustani. I wasn't never good at the language, and I only managed to get hold of a word here and there. As far as I could make it out they was talking about this stone. I heard the blackie keep on saying, "Give it up and you shall go safe." He'd hark back to that whenever 'e couldn't think of anything else to say. Well, after about 'arf an hour of his 'igh-class patter he seemed to think the time 'ad come for a bit of knockabout business. He ups with his hand and shouts something, and at us they all come in a body. It was gettin' pretty dark then, or they wouldn't have risked a frontal attack. I loosed off with my revolver and bowled over the blackie who'd been doing the talking – hit him on the ankle. Then they all came on, yelling and firing, and matters became a little 'ot. Down goes the Major with a bullet in the shoulder, and, just as I'm beginning to think it's all up, out comes the moon, and it's like daylight. That settled their 'ash. They couldn't see me, and I could see them proper. I 'ad three of 'em down and out before you could say knife, and that conclooded the proceedings. They sheered off, taking the boss blackie with them, and didn't come back no more. I tied the Major's shoulder up and did wot I could for him, and when he was a bit easier he calls me, and says, "Burrows." "Sir?" I says. He 'ands me the blue ruin. "Wot's this sir?" I says. "Never mind," he says. "It's valuable. You must go on with it alone. I shall 'ave to stay here and mend. Guard that stone with your bloomin' life, and 'and it over to Colonel Stewart in England.'

'By Jingo!' said Tommy. It was the first time he had spoken.

'You did splendidly, Burrows. I'll see that official notice is taken of what you have done. And now I'll add my information to yours. This is the Tear of Heaven. You'll read about it in any good book on India. It is the sacred jewel of the Maharajahs of Estapore. The people of the state believe the stone to be sacred and worship it. Without it a Maharajah would have little chance of keeping his throne. Now in Estapore things are more than a little complicated. In these native states the ruler can name his heir. The succession does not go automatically to the eldest son. And that is the trouble in Estapore. The old Maharajah has two sons, and the younger is the one he has named as his heir. Naturally the elder son is jealous, and when an oriental is jealous things are likely to happen. So the Maharajah consulted me. I advised him to send the heir to England to be educated, which he did. He went to Eton, and later to Cambridge, where he is now. You probably know his name quite well. He got his cricket blue last season.'

Jimmy and Tommy gave a simultaneous gasp.

'Not the chap who made a century against Oxford?'

The Colonel nodded and went on.

'Having got him out of the country he was safe as long as his father lived. If he had remained at Estapore he would have been murdered as sure as we are sitting here. But now, I suspect, the old Maharajah feels himself nearing the end, and is anxious to make preparations that will ensure his heir succeeding to the throne. That is where the stone comes in. In a nutshell, the position is this. The man who has the stone gets the throne, for the people, whatever their political views, would be absolutely swayed by their superstition. They would no more dare to oppose the owner of the sacred stone than fly. So the old Maharajah gave this stone to Ingram to take to me, the guardian of the heir. If I had been at home all would have been simple. I should have handed the stone to the heir, and he would have returned with it, strongly guarded, to Estapore, for, you must know, it is greatly to the interest of Britain that your friend the cricketer should succeed to the throne.'

He paused.

'By Jingo!' said Tommy.

'But, father,' said Jimmy, 'how did Spinder know that the stone meant such a lot?'

'Spinder? Spinder? A small man with a hooked nose? Wears glasses?'

'Yes, yes.'

'It must be the same. Why, this Mr Spinder is one of the best-informed men on Indian mythology in the country. He would have read all about the Tear of Heaven in the course of his studies. I suppose he recognised the stone and was holding it up to ransom when they took it by force.'

'And who was Marshall?'

'And Ferris?' added Tommy.

'Agents of the usurper. Probably broken army men who had got mixed up in shady affairs. There are scores of them in the underworld of India. And now,' said the Colonel, 'you two boys had better be running off, or you will be late for school.'

Subsequent revelations proved that the Colonel was right. The Indian who had perished in the motor smash was the claimant to the throne of Estapore. His death made the rest of the affair simple.

To Tommy and Jimmy the rest of the term seemed terribly flat and uninteresting after the excitement they had gone through.

THE END

# TITLES IN THE EVERYMAN WODEHOUSE